THE GENTLE

CONQUISTADORS

The Ten Year Odyssey

Across the American Southwest

of Three Spanish Captains and

Esteban, a Black Slave

JEANNETTE MIRSKY

Illustrated by Thomas Morley

Kaye & Ward, London

For Anne Guthrie with admiration and love

First published in the United Kingdom by Kaye & Ward Ltd,
1972.

ISBN 0 7182 0765 3

All inquiries and requests relevant to this title should be
sent to the publisher, Kaye & Ward Ltd, London EC2,
and not to the printer.

Reproduced and printed in Great Britain by
Redwood Press Limited
Trowbridge & London

FRANCE

ATLANTIC OCEAN

SPAIN

PORTUGAL

Estremadura

*Sevilla

Gran*ada

Gibraltar

Palos de la Frontera
Sanlucar de Barrameda

Azamor
*

MEDITERRANEAN SEA

MOROCCO

ary Islands

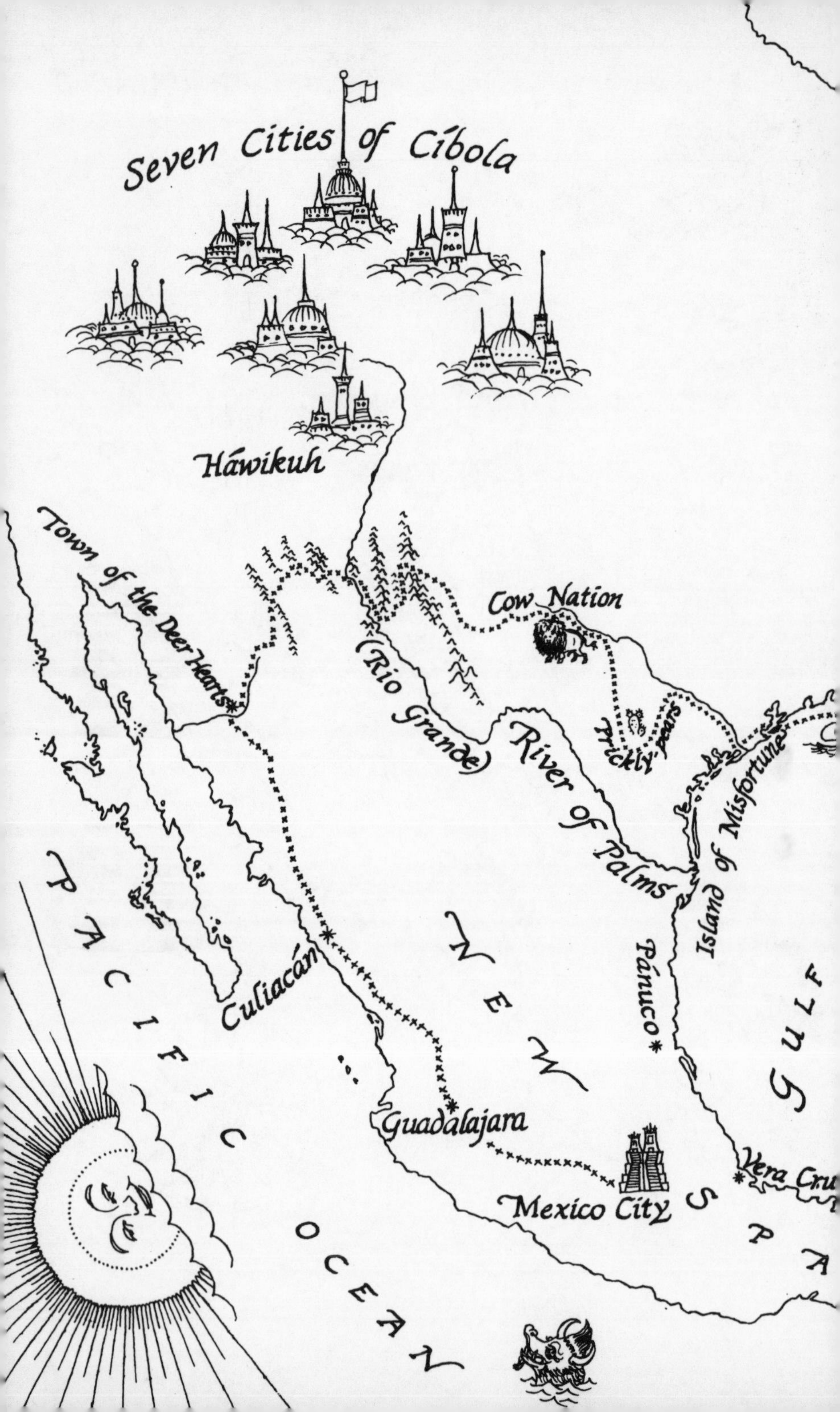
Seven Cities of Cíbola
Háwikuh
Town of the Deer Hearts
Cow Nation
(Rio Grande)
River of Palms
Prickly pears
Island of Misfortune
Culiacán
Pánuco
Guadalajara
Mexico City
Vera Cru
PACIFIC OCEAN
NEW
SPA
GULF

ATLANTIC

OCEAN

LA FLORIDA

Apalache
Aute
Bay of Horses

MEXICO

CUBA

Santiago de Cuba

Santo Domingo

CARIBBEAN SEA

1/Before the Beginning

THE PIRATE SHIP sailing out of the Mediterranean through the Straits of Gilbraltar responded to the swells of the Atlantic. The motion woke the young man from his sleep, a light, fitful, uneasy sleep. Asleep or awake he was caught in the same nightmare. He turned over to ease the anguish that gripped him and immediately the chain on his leg clanked. The rattle told him: You are a captive; you will be sold as a slave.

From now on, no moving about, no work was his to decide to do; from now on, his legs and arms and hands would do what another person ordered. No longer would he look at the sun to see what the hour was—what did it matter what the sun told him, since time itself was now no longer his to spend.

What will it be like to be a slave, he asked himself bitterly. Property? Belonging to someone? He closed his eyes. He had to find a way out of the bewilderment and helplessness that exhausted him.

The dazed shock was lessening. The pirates had swooped down so suddenly, so unexpectedly. In one brutal, violent moment he had ceased being a passenger, a modest trader who had paid for deck space on a vessel, and become a captive: pirate loot. How long ago was it? Hours or days—what did it matter.

His mind ran far and fast from his despair. He thought of his childhood. He wondered if anything would ever again be so bright and carefree. Thoughts of his boyhood brought thoughts of his father, a tall, dignified, proud man respected for his honesty. He was one of the merchants who sold the dried fish for which Azamor was famous. His customers in the many little settlements along the Moroccan coast looked forward to his trading visits —he brought them news of other places and he also offered helpful suggestions when his advice was asked. His father had loved him; when he was home they were much together. He grew easier thinking about his boyhood.

If he had not loved his father so much, he never would have run away from the catastrophe that overwhelmed Azamor. He was still a boy, almost a man, when the Portuguese ships had appeared outside the harbour. It was the second time. The first time, five years earlier, he remembered well, and the excitement that had gripped Azamor. On their first try, the Portuguese flotilla had been caught and swamped in the mighty breakers that crashed on the sandbar. Hundreds of heavily armoured soldiers had drowned and their pale bodies had washed up on the shore.

The townspeople felt triumphant at the victory the breakers had won for them. They thought they were quite secure. "The Nazarenes," for so they called the Christians, "do not know the channel; they will never be able to slip through the barrier of the waves—alive."

But his father knew better. He had heard of treachery at other towns, towns that also had reason to feel secure. "It is only the water that is spilt; the ewer is not broken," he told all who would listen to him, using an old proverb. And when they still would not make any attempt to defend themselves, he said straight out, "This is a warning to be heeded. They will come again and again until they succeed."

He told his son what he wanted him to do, and why. "The Nazarenes want to conquer the world. One little defeat will not stop them. I am too old to begin life over again. You are young; you are smart, quick, and resourceful. You can make your life elsewhere. As soon as their ships appear again, I want you to run to safety. Go to the hills. If they fail again, you can return; but if they succeed—" His hands dropped, his shoulders sagged, but his voice was firm. "From there you will find a place where the Nazarenes will not come."

His father drew him close to him. "As you love me, as you respect me, promise you will do as I ask." The boy nodded; he felt the solemnity of the occasion. "I do not want you to be killed or made a slave." His mother watched and listened, but said nothing.

After that, often when the Nazarenes were mentioned, his father would repeat his hope that his son would not suffer death or enslavement. It made escape not a cowardly act but rather a difficult one he must do to please his father. And so, when the successful attempt came, the sight of Portuguese ships massed outside the sandbar brought father and son together in their home. No explanations were needed; everything but the farewells had been said. The boy knew his father's wish.

Quickly his mother strung some dried fish so he would have food to sustain him and filled a calabash with water, pressing the sweet-grass stopper firmly in. Quickly his father blessed him, gave him a kiss on his forehead, and held him close for a moment. The last thing he felt was his mother's soft pat on the cheek. Without a word he started walking swiftly toward the hills. He dared not look back.

He sobbed as he walked. The pain of parting—he had never known so sharp and heavy a pain before. His love for his father gave him the strength to go on. The farewell had been so sudden, so brief; but soon he began to understand that his preparation for such a flight had been a long, loving farewell. Hours later, when he had gained the hilltop, he turned and saw far below and at a distance a high, black cloud of smoke rising above Azamor.

How terrible, how bitter had been his loss—his father and mother probably dead. Azamor in ashes. And himself—? A wanderer, a refugee like so many others, dependent on people's charity. He did what he could to repay the kindnesses shown him and little by little managed to earn his way. As he grew in independence he knew how precious was the legacy his father had given him: He was alive, he was free.

"Free," he thought quietly and put the thought away, able to face the truth. "Now that I shall be a slave I must do as my father would have urged. I must not be afraid to live." He did not think of courage and confidence, but only resolved to live unafraid. His life had been disrupted once, and though it had been hard, it had been interesting to see the world as a trader. "Now," he thought, "I may see stranger things as a slave."

He sat up.

The wind that blew had the ocean freshness he knew so well from Azamor; it flowed lightly over his skin. He had but to close his eyes and feel his mother's hand stroking him as she whispered his name. "Talisman, Talisman." So she had named him. "You have brought me all that is good. Even a slave can have good luck." And her face would light up in a smile.

She was a slave. She was young when he was born, a little Black Songhai girl who had been caught by slaveraiders and brought across the Sahara to Morocco. His father had bought her to do the gutting and drying of fish. She became the mother of his only son—the houses of his wives were filled with daughters. The wives found it hard to hate her, for she had the gentle, happy nature of her people. And a deep wisdom of her own. If she had given herself airs, been mean or stingy, they could have schemed against her; instead they came gladly to her hut when she invited them to share a potful of stew, big chunks of fish swimming in a delicious hot sauce seasoned with peppers as she had learned to cook in her mother's house. "People who eat from the same pot are friends," she had said. It was his mother who brought peace to his father's house.

Thinking of her, remembering her rich, tasty food made him smile with happiness. His smile—warm, pleasant, and open like hers—attracted people; they felt his good nature and liked having him around.

His father, his mother, both had pride. Yet how different, how very different the pride was. His father's was part of the authority he commanded; it was like a splendidly embroidered gown worn to catch the beholder's eye. Hers, on the contrary, was a secret strength, a hidden coat of mail which no hurt could pierce. He remembered a scene when he had been old enough to feel the indignity she suffered but was still too young to protect her. It had been a brutal day, and the hot wind from the desert scorched the lungs and made breathing an effort. He was walking with his mother when a woman—he never knew the reason she did it—called her "slave."

His mother had taken his hand to bring him closer to her, and without saying a word, without looking hurt or crushed, unhurriedly had walked away. He knew what a slave was—there were men and women, and there were slaves. His mother had often used the word, but never before had he heard anyone call her that. When they were alone, he asked her, "Why did she insult you?"

"She didn't."

"She called you a slave."

"That is not an insult. I am a slave."

For a while he was silent as he considered this. Then he asked, "What does it feel like to be a slave?"

"Let me see how I can answer that," she said. After a brief silence, speaking slowly, carefully, thoughtfully, she continued. "I am a slave. I was captured and sold to your father. He is my master. He has never called me a slave. I have learned that some people feel better if they try to treat me like one." Then she repeated his question: "What does it feel like to be a slave? I have never felt like one. No one has ever been able to make me feel like a slave." Then the seriousness fled from her face as she smiled. "I can tell you how it feels to be a mother," and she hugged him close to her.

He never forgot her words, rather he kept thinking about them, turning them this way and that in his mind, examining them deeply. Now more than ever before they were vivid and relevant; they told him something he needed badly to know. He closed his eyes against the morning light so that he could recall the moment more intensely. With her example to guide him, he vowed he would not let himself feel like a slave. He could almost feel his mother—and then with a start he roused himself from his drowsy state. The body he felt was real. The man next to him had stirred, doubling up to smother a groan. It was the rich merchant who had occupied the only cabin on the seized vessel. The man on his other side, lying straight and still, stared ahead with unseeing eyes. He had been one of the sailors. Like pendants hanging from a chain, the captives were strung out along the deck,

rich and poor, possessed of nothing but the clothes they wore and the small space their bodies needed. Chained together they were equal in their misfortune.

He closed his eyes to blot out the misery around him. For an instant the groan brought back his own fears and despair. And then he realized that nothing is gained by lamenting what cannot be changed. Some day, yes, but not now. It was not lamentation that was needed, but courage and spirit to face whatever came. "No one has ever been able to make me feel like a slave." He repeated his mother's words over and over like a spell. Nobody but a slave can give advice to a slave; he began to understand the dignity of what she had told him.

He looked at his companions. Were they asleep or still stunned? Or were they, like himself, lying motionless while their thoughts raced in all directions seeking ways to accommodate to their new state?

"Allah, be merciful." It was a sigh that came from somewhere along the line of captives.

The morning sun shone just above the ship's stern when a pirate brought each man a mug and some hard sea biscuits; after him came another, ladling out water. Chatting to each other, they looked carefully at their prisoners, ready at a sign to give more biscuits and water.

"They obey the injunction that says 'The good farmer is one who is good to his animals,' " said the merchant sourly. "They tend us as I had my asses and camels cared for."

"What tongue do these infidels speak?" The question

came from a wiry man whose arm was wrapped in a bloody rag.

"I only know the language of the Genoese," the merchant volunteered. "Theirs is different."

"It is akin to that of the Portuguese," said the young man from Azamor. "I have been listening and I understand some of their words. Perhaps," he added, "they speak the tongue of those who come from Andalusia, the kingdom next to Portugal."

"What does it matter what they speak?" the wounded man asked. "We shall have to learn their words quickly otherwise they will shout at us as if we were deaf." He added bitterly, "We shall also learn what each of us is worth."

"Tell me, merchant, how do you set the price of a man?" the sailor asked.

Thrown back into their private despairs, the prisoners fell silent. Miserable, they sat and watched as hour after hour the ship, following the coast, sailed northwestward. The ship flew before a brisk breeze, and the mountains fell away sharply. They passed glittering sand dunes which edged an undulating plain of low-lying hills separated by large meadows of salt marshes. Fishing boats appeared in increasing numbers, and the pirates waved to each and halloed. They were happy. They were bringing in a good catch; they had met no real enemies; the winds had favoured them, and in a matter of hours they would be in port. The sun was low in the sky.

"It is the hour for prayer," said the merchant, who was pious as well as rich. "But how shall we pray?" He spoke out loud, not to his fellow Muslims but to God. "Allah, be merciful. I cannot cleanse myself properly to be fit for prayer. I cannot prostrate myself with this chain on my leg. I do not even know which way to face. In what direction lies holy Mecca? Allah, be merciful." He repeated it again and again.

Even as he was praying and complaining the ship turned toward the land. It entered a river that met the sea without a ripple, and sailed between shores lined with tall plumed grasses. The smell of land, of vegetation rank and rich, told the captives that soon they would disembark.

There was no sound and hardly any movement as the ship advanced up the tidal river to where the hills rose. The autumn evening was soft; air and earth and water lay under an immense peace. Only the sky was red, as though smeared with blood.

SLAVES, SLAVES!" The cry ran ahead of them and the crowds parted to let them pass.

The prisoners walked slowly, stiff from their confinement on the ship and encumbered by the dragging chain. Joined leg to leg in a long line, they stumbled toward the slave compound.

Night lay over the land. In the town, flares burning outside the houses lighted the streets and alleys in which people jostled and swarmed. After the silent emptiness of the sea, the prisoners were unprepared for such bustle and noise. The target of hundreds of eyes and of words hurled at them whose meaning they could not understand, they stared back, too amazed to be self-conscious.

Never had they seen so many and such an assortment of Nazarenes! Seafaring men, ruddy from exposure to wind and sun, walked as though a pitching deck were still underfoot; sober men, sea captains and pilots, strolled arm-in-arm, aware of their own importance; monks and priests in sombre habits mixed with all groups; adventurers and soldiers of fortune swaggered in their silken finery. Men spilled out of the wine shops to look, and so did buxom girls, who stood in twos and threes, unveiled and unashamed. And darting in and out were poor, ragged men, beggars and cripples; silent men, white and gaunt and shaking from foreign fevers, leaned against doorways; while here and there, like exotic flowers, were Indians, naked men of strange mien from the New World. They moved with a stately presence and many wore splendid bright feathers and large golden ornaments.

The pirates had put into Palos de la Frontera. Formerly a centre of Spain's African slave trade, the port had known a dozen lean years when a treaty with Portugal forbade the trade to Spaniards. And then had come the memorable, miraculous first voyage of the Genoese, Columbus. In the more than thirty years since, many ships had followed his path across the Ocean Sea—most licensed by the king, some sailing secretly, illegally. Thousands of Spaniards—fighters, fortune hunters, and all kinds of colonists—crowded the ports waiting for space and a chance. Restless, charged with hope, they shared a single thought: to become part of the great New World adventure.

They had good cause to be eager. Only a few years before, Cortés had realized the dreams of all young, brash, impecunious adventurers who asked to be given the chance to gamble their lives for fame and fortune. Cortés had not only worsted the powerful Governor of Cuba but he had also won an empire! A New World, a New Spain—and always gold, gold, gold. Men had left without a copper and returned with fabulous riches. Gold and silver, pearls and slaves were the chief topics that commanded their thoughts and tongues.

The prisoners felt the vigour that possessed the town. They had no need to know the language to understand the excitement; their ears caught it in the too-loud laughter and the boisterous tone of the voices. The young man from Azamor responded to this liveliness. An upsurge of hope filled his heart. "A slave," he repeated his mother's words to himself as if to justify his response, "even a slave can have good luck."

He kept thinking hard and fast. "No one can force me to feel like a slave. If I had chosen to come to this town to trade, I would like this stir. I would look around for customers." The chain on his leg held him firmly in line. "If my feet cannot go where they want to, my eyes can. Somewhere, maybe, one of the faces I see will be that of my master. Which one? Which one? Perhaps I can find him." His eyes looked to the right and left, scanning the groups, searching among the faces. "I will probably fetch a very high price," he thought without pride but with the cool head of a trader. "What kind of man can afford me?" His eye was caught by some dandies who lolled at a table, conscious of their satin splendour."My master will be such a one, a young, untried dandy whose appearance means more to him than his money. Not a fool," he corrected himself sensing their empty vanity. "Not a weakling who must have a slave to make himself feel superior."

Walking along, his thoughts followed his eyes, glad of the game he could play; it pushed out the terrible uncertainty of his impending fate.

And then a mysterious impulse—he never forgot its urgent nature—made him turn his head sharply toward a young man who stood apart from the throng, earnestly talking to a short, older man. He could not make out his features which were hidden in the shadow of the flares. Even as he was looking, the Spaniard jerked his head up and turned toward him. For a moment, across the tumble of heads, their eyes met.

ANDRES DORANTES DE CARRANCA had come down the river to Palos from his lodgings in nearby Gibraleon to consult his cousin, the influential chief of the Palos port. Born into a fairly well-to-do family, a younger son, he was in search of his fortune. Like many others he had been gently reared, and like them, he too was penniless because the law of primogeniture made the firstborn son the sole heir. For centuries bands of younger sons had fought the Moors in Spain in order to possess their wealth and lands. With the fall of Granada, the last of the Moorish kingdoms, this way of earning a living ended. For them, Columbus's discovery meant a new world and a new opportunity. And so these younger sons, restless, ambitious, bred to regard fighting as the only way to acquire riches and estates, became the conquistadors who swarmed over vast stretches of the New World.

Dorantes walked toward the port. Taller than most, he moved through the crowds with the easy, alert grace of a fencer. Already he had made a name for himself in this art, a useful and commendable reputation to have. He had come to Palos to learn the latest news and gossip, especially to sift the rumours of a new expedition. Looking around, he caught sight of his cousin standing outside the customs building.

"Don Pedro," he called out. His cousin smiled when he saw him. Don Pedro was proud of his cousin's skill with the sword and respected him for not wasting his time and talent in senseless duelling.

"Andrés, I am glad to see you. You are lucky you did not come yesterday. I returned from Seville late last night." Pedro de Carranca's manner showed the affection he felt. "I have important news for you."

"What? Have you found me an heiress?" Dorantes was amused at his cousin's efforts on his behalf.

"I didn't think you needed me for that. But enough nonsense. I was going to send for you. There is a great new expedition which you should join."

"What a coincidence," Dorantes said. "I am here to find out about it. The whole country is full of rumours."

"Rumours, rumours, they are as plentiful as fleas," Don Pedro said, shaking his head. "What I have to tell you is straight from Seville and the court. His Sacred Majesty has given a grant for La Florida, the same land discovered by the ill-fated Ponce de León. The expedition will be magnificent, worthy of so valuable a grant." His voice carried the excitement of the prospect of a mighty venture, and he did not want his young cousin to miss this opportunity.

"So far you have not told me anything more than the rumours. Tell me what you know, please."

"I have seen the grant itself. Studied it. It covers the region between the Cape of Florida and the River of Palms, whose mouth is close to Pánuco, Cortés's new settlement along the east coast, a very handsome size. It is given to be conquered and governed. It will be the finest venture yet sent out. It is ideal for you—important, noble, bound to be successful."

Dorantes said nothing; he listened to hear if his cousin would mention the part of the news that had disturbed him. The chief of the port looked at him as if he had said everything that was important.

"I know you have been preparing yourself for something like this. I've seen how you listen to what the men have to say when ships from the Western Islands return. You have heard their stories—sometimes they are stirring, sometimes terrible and heartbreaking. Always they speak of treasure and marvels. I can assure you, I have checked and double-checked: there is some truth in what they relate, no matter how preposterous it sounds.

"Remember when they unloaded baskets filled with pearls? And the incredibly coloured birds they had? I have even been privileged to taste royal delicacies—pineapples and potatoes pickled in wine." His enthusiasm collapsed, and he added solicitously, "You have also surely learned that the New World demands courage and stamina, great will, and most of all, God's grace."

Dorantes interrupted him, "What about that peacock Narváez?" As he blurted out that name his cousin sensed the crux of his misgivings.

"Don Pánfilo de Narváez," Carranca gave the full name in a sonorous official tone, "has pledged his own fortune as well as his wife's—one of the greatest in Spain in case you do not know it—to make the expedition glorious. He means to equip and supply six hundred recruits. He will stint on nothing. Nothing."

Undaunted, Dorantes pursued the conversation. "Rumours say a dozen men, rich, well-placed, experienced, tried to secure the royal grant. Yet it was given to Narváez. Why? He has already shown that he is lacking in caution. Why give such a plum to that One-Eyed One?"

"That question will not get you to the New World. Nor will insults." His cousin spoke tartly. And then in a friendly manner he said, "I do not blame you for asking that. You are not the only one. In fact," and he looked around to see he was not overheard, "in Seville they say Narváez has learned to be careful—he never lets the king see that he lost an eye to Cortés." The two men laughed at this joke together.

"Tell me, Don Pedro, what happened to Narváez in Mexico. I never heard the real story. No one seems to be willing to talk about it. Was it so disgraceful?"

"All right, I'll tell you. Even the worst truth is better than the worst rumours." Carranca spoke quickly and to the point. "Narváez's patron, the powerful governor of Cuba, entrusted him with a very considerable force and sent him to Mexico to stop Cortés. The governor considered Cortés an upstart; he wanted Mexico to be wholly his prize. In the struggle between the peacock Narváez and Cortés, the fox, the bird lost his troops to the wily fox, who persuaded them to desert, and when they met in combat, he also lost an eye and his liberty. It was as Cortés's prisoner that Don Pánfilo visited Mexico City. Imagine the humiliation. Nevertheless, he returned to Spain as cocky as if nothing had happened. 'The peacock lost an eye but not his tail feathers,' his enemies said."

After a pause Carranca finished his story. "I'll agree it takes a certain talent not to know when you fail so utterly. However, I am certain that as governor, Don Pánfilo will act quite differently: he will be his own master. Andrés, do not question the king's wisdom; no good comes of that. And remember that Narváez is known to have been a brave fighter against the Indians. He is fearless, and above all, honest."

"Since when does honesty, a quality expected of a

gentleman, become a virtue to be singled out and ap-
plauded?" Dorantes remained unconvinced of Narváez's
fitness.

Carranca did not try to answer his cousin. He had kept
his most telling argument for the last. "I counsel you to
join. Since the news has leaked out, cadets from the best
families are flocking to Seville. I have learned from the
highest sources that there will be enough treasure and
positions of power to satisfy all. My own reason for urging you is this: Vaca, the same Cabeza de Vaca with
whom I became close friends when we served under the
Duke of Medina Sidonia, has been named second in command. He is the Treasurer and High Sheriff.

"Go to Vaca. He will help you for our friendship's
sake. Andrés, I'll wager any sum you want that Vaca
will prove his exceptional qualities in La Florida."

As his cousin was encouraging him, at the very moment that Vaca's name was mentioned, Dorantes felt a
mysterious impulse. Later, he would have taken an oath
that he heard his name called. Raising his eyes to where
the sound seemed to come from, he saw a black face looking fixedly at him. He felt a searching look.

"I think I will," he said after a moment.

"Will what?"

"Oh, I just decided to buy a slave. Might be useful on
the expedition."

"What a foolish way to announce you have made up
your mind. Anyway, I am glad. Were I younger, I would
join the expedition." Carranca was pleased that he had
persuaded his cousin. "Go with God."

THE NEXT MORNING the two men went to the slave compound; though it adjoined the customs building, Dorantes had never been inside it before. "It looks," he thought as he entered, "like a sheep corral—but there is a difference between sheep and men: the sheep always bunch together, but the slaves stand apart, each one alone, separate." He did not quite know what he was seeking when, without hesitation, he pointed to the slave he sought. Still under the powerful impulse of the previous night, he asked no question, not the man's name, whence he came, his skills: nothing but his price. It was high. To pay it Dorantes borrowed from his cousin, promising, as was customary, to pay back ten times the amount when he returned from La Florida a rich man. As soon as the sale papers were signed and notarized, master and slave prepared to start for Seville where the expedition wàs being recruited.

"Don Pedro, I knew you would be very helpful, but your generosity leaves me your debtor for far more than the loan you made. I thank you for everything." Dorantes's voice showed the emotion he felt. "I shall seek out your friend Vaca. If I don't return you can collect from my brother. I shall write and ask him to do me this one favour."

"I'm not worried. You will return and make me a rich man. But how are you going? You must buy a horse. By the road it's almost two hundred miles to Seville."

"We need the walk to stretch our legs. If I am permitted to join, we shall be cramped long enough on the ship.

And anyway, unless we have two horses we won't make any better time. We are both travelling light. I'll get my gear when I'm certain I'm going."

Having bid his cousin farewell, master and slave took the road to Seville.

For a long time they did not speak. They found their strides matched, a long, easy, effortless stride that carried them mile after mile. There was a kind of shyness that inhibited their talking. Neither had had previous experience in his role—Dorantes had never been a master and the man from Azamor had never been a slave. This inexperience gave them an unexpected equality as each tried to assess the other. Then Dorantes found that his slave's Portuguese made it possible for them to talk together.

"What are you called?" Dorantes took the lead in asking questions.

"By whom?"

Dorantes was not prepared for this answer. Was his slave going to be sulky and evasive? Looking at him, he saw a genuine puzzlement on his face.

"What do you mean, by whom? By your father and mother, of course."

"My father called me Hassan, my mother Tilsam, which in your language means Talisman."

"Hassan is a Muslim name." Dorantes paused and then asked, "Are you of that faith?"

"Islam was the religion of my father," the slave answered straightforwardly, and then added, "but my mother was a pagan who knew nothing of Allah. 'Unbelieving Dog' is the Muslim's name for such." And then the slave added softly and without animosity, "It is also the name we use for Nazarenes."

"And you? Of what belief are you? Are you, like your mother, an Unbelieving Dog?" Dorantes was frankly curious.

"I suppose I must consider myself partly that," the slave answered with dignity. "I believed when my mother spoke of a mighty spirit. Her god had no name, the word she used simply means all-wise creator. At the same time I learned from my father that there is no God but Allah and Muhammed is His Prophet. When I was a child at home, it was easy to reconcile the two beliefs. I decided that my mother's all-wise creator and my father's Allah were the same; the difference was in the language. I my- self had different names—why shouldn't God?"

"But you are not a child now," Dorantes said.

"That's true. But neither am I in the land of my child- hood. Against my will I was brought to the land of the Nazarenes." He looked at his master, who listened atten- tively. "What does that mean, you will ask? I will answer truthfully. It is for you to understand beyond my poor words." Dorantes nodded and looked intently at this man whom he had bought.

The man from Azamor continued. "While I lay chained on the deck, wondering what my new life would bring, I thought of the Nazarenes captured by my people. There are many such among us. They all accepted Islam; whether out of fear or faith I cannot say. But I do know that once they became Muslims, they became part of the life around them." He paused, and as an afterthought added, "I never asked them what they believed."

Dorantes listened and his silence encouraged the slave to continue. "Master, if I understood rightly we are bound on a great adventure. Whether we come back or not is in the hands of God. We must, of course, do our best to live —that is our duty as human beings. But as for who God is, I see the great truth in our proverb."

"What is the proverb on which you will stake your soul?" Dorantes, a good Christian, asked.

"God, we say, has a hundred names. Man knows ninety-nine. Only the camel knows all one hundred."

"When we get near Seville, I shall present you to a camel," Dorantes said. They smiled at each other. They had forged a bond—it left them tired.

In the following days Dorantes was delighted when he realized how quick his slave was in learning Spanish. Already he was using words and phrases and constantly seeking to extend his familiarity with the new language.

Outside Seville they stopped at a monastery where Dorantes presented his slave to a thin, dark, intense man. "He looks," thought the man from Azamor, "like one of my countrymen."

"Brother Sebastián taught me when I was a child. He is the son of a *converso*—his father was a Moor who was baptized a Christian after we conquered Granada. He speaks your tongue. He is a good man and you will learn to honour him as I do. He will instruct you in the true faith."

They had, they found to their dismay, plenty of time to talk and learn. At first Dorantes was caught up in the excitement of Seville and the pleasant hospitality of the monastery which was almost like a second home. But as autumn passed he began to fret: Narváez repeatedly put off coming to Seville, preferring to enjoy the attention his high appointment won him and the festivities given to honour his departure. Each time Narváez's arrival was postponed, Dorantes grew more impatient. Was he or was he not going to be invited to join the expedition?

It was mid-winter when Vaca, without warning, visited Seville, coming from Sanlúcar de Barrameda, Seville's port, seventy-five miles down the river, where he had been overseeing the victualling and equipping of the fleet. Mindful of his cousin's advice, Dorantes took this opportunity to present himself to the expedition's second-in-command.

Vaca made him instantly welcome—for Carranca had written his old comrade-in-arms a glowing account of his cousin's qualities—and promised to recommend him to Narváez. Confident that this was as good as an acceptance, Dorantes decided to leave Seville, find lodgings in Sanlúcar, and begin assembling his wardrobe and gear. He knew the news that Cabeza de Vaca had treated him as a friend would spread fast and far; this fact as well as his being rich enough to own a slave would make it easy for him to obtain credit from landlords and outfitters. His future looked certain and rosy.

Walking back to the monastery Dorantes said to his slave, "Brother Sebastián will be delighted to hear what Vaca promised. I'm sure he knows Vaca. He will tell me if my impression of the man is right or not. Also, before I leave tomorrow morning, I want to hear mass in his chapel."

"Master," said the man from Azamor, "I too have news that will please him. When we were first on our way to the monastery, you said I would learn to honour Brother Sebastián. I have. I do. Step by step he has shown me the path he took to come home to God's infinite love and mercy. He did more than teach me the catechism: he planted its meaning in my heart. I want you to know this because you are the one who gave me the chance to find myself. It is just as my mother used to say, 'even a slave can have good luck.' " He stopped and looked at Dorantes, "Don Andrés, I want to become a Christian."

Dorantes looked hard at the man he had bought, moved as much by the simple dignity of his manner as by the words he had spoken. "That will give the good brother great joy. I am happy, very happy that you do it out of your own faith and wish. We will be able to hear mass together."

Brother Sebastián showed his pleasure at the good news each had to tell him. Relaxing after the first rush of words, they chatted of this and that, at ease with the solutions made after long waiting and aware that this was the night before they parted.

"Really, every time I say it, I think what a ridiculous name Cabeza de Vaca is," Dorantes remarked.

"But it's his mother's family name," Brother Sebastián said as if that explained everything. "He was christened Álvar Núñez. Like everyone else he had a choice of family names. His mother's comes from the ancestor who long ago found an unknown mountain pass and marked it with a cow's skull. He made it possible for the Christians to surprise and rout the Moors. The name celebrates a notable victory. Equally, of course, he could have been 'de Vera,' his father's family name. Álvar Núñez is the grandson of *the* Pedro de Vera—most often called the Illustrious Vera." The brother's voice had a sarcastic ring.

"Easy, easy. I heard a trace of hate as you said that," Dorantes said with mock severity. "And you wearing the habit of the gentle Saint Francis."

"You are right, my son. To hate is evil—a sin. I thought I was expressing righteous anger when I spoke of Vera, conqueror of the Canary Islands. From brother Franciscans I heard that Don Pedro de Vera had a devil in him that took pleasure in inflicting pain. He did dreadful things, needlessly dreadful, to the defenceless savages. And it *is* my duty to condemn the atrocities he committed. Please notice, however, that though Vaca speaks proudly of his grandfather, he did not choose to bear his name. To me, Andrés, that is his grandson's way of passing judgement."

"I understand. But still, a soldier harbouring such noble sensibilities! Was he not shaken by the slaughter at the Battle of Ravenna—where twenty thousand men died? Yet my cousin tells me that Vaca distinguished himself there." Thinking it over, Dorantes shook his head. "To be a good soldier and also a human being filled with compassion—a very rare combination. Somehow it wins my admiration. I'm glad he will be second in command. I like him."

The slave from Azamor listened. When they had finished he said, "As a trader, my livelihood depended on judging whom I could trust. Your Vaca is slight, but his body is like Spanish steel, strong, tough, resilient and enduring. Also, like the best steel, he is handsome."

"I keep seeing him as he was when I called on him," Dorantes said. "He was checking lists, paying attention to every detail of the supplies which had been ordered. When he had verified the very last item, he said by way of explanation, 'I must make sure that we will get what we are paying for. Misfortune is the inevitable price paid for carelessness and poor planning.' I like such caution in a man of action. Brother Sebastián, I think Vaca is warmhearted and not hot-headed," Dorantes added, pleased at the way he summed it up.

When Brother Sebastián had left them, the slave said to Dorantes, "I too felt that Vaca was stern but without any hardness in his nature. I kept noticing how carefully he listened when you talked about yourself; how he observed you. Nothing escapes his eye. He is, like my father was, a just man; a man to be relied on."

T HE NEXT MORNING before they left for Sanlúcar, the man from Azamor was baptized. Dorantes stood as his godfather. Brother Sebastián, deeply touched that this young, black stranger, whose seriousness and manliness had impressed him during all their conversations—a most worthy soul to have been able to sáve—

wanted to carry his name when he came into the Christian fold.

When the baptism was over and they had heard mass, they stood outside the church waiting for Brother Sebastián to join them. "It's too confusing having two Sebastiáns," Dorantes said. "I christen thee by the nickname Esteban."

"Two baptisms within the hour. Doesn't that give me some kind of record," Esteban said, adding, "before today I was only half an Unbelieving Dog; now I am wholly one." And they laughed easily together at their private joke.

"You have chosen your name with wisdom and forethought," Brother Sebastián said, blessing them as they were leaving. "May the good Saint Sebastián protect both of you from the arrows of the Indians."

2 | The Expedition

VACA WAS AS GOOD as his word. As soon as Narváez came to Sanlúcar from Seville, he arranged to present Dorantes to him. He managed to say quite casually that the young man's cousin was chief of the port of Palos and that he already had a reputation as a fencer.

For this important audience, Dorantes dressed in his newest and finest garments. He wore only a dagger—his sword was carried by Esteban, who followed him. His style impressed Narváez.

"Don Andrés Dorantes de Carranca, I bid you welcome." Narváez was a tall, heavy-set man of impressive bearing and his voice was deep and resonating. In manner and dress he was already governor of the golden La Florida. "It pleases me greatly to have you as one of our company. Your noble birth and your swordsmanship have earned you a commission: You will serve as a captain of infantry." Dorantes bowed, pleased at his appointment.

"Also," Narváez continued, "when we reach La Florida I shall need you as one of the company of men of gentle breeding to accompany me when I meet Datha, King of Chicora. Have you heard about that royal giant?"

"No, my lord."

"Ah, yes, the news is most recent and not widely known. Most extraordinary, most interesting. Let me tell you about him. Pray, be seated." Esteban stood behind Dorantes's chair. "I heard about him from that great authority, Peter Martyr, God rest his soul. Alas, that he died before his brilliant pen could chronicle our conquest of La Florida. Then all Europe would know about it. Have you read Peter Martyr?"

"Yes, my lord. From him I learned about the New World and all its many marvels."

"Good, very good. Peter Martyr explained how Datha attained his monstrous size. He does not come from a race of giants. Quite the contrary. But from infancy on, he was daily rubbed with the juice of a certain plant, then massaged and stretched. Incredible? Yet by such treatment all the royal heirs become giants. Martyr was told this by a subject of Datha's who was converted to Christianity."

"Permit me to inquire of your excellency if Datha's is the kingdom famous for its immense riches in gold and exceedingly large pearls?"

"The same, Don Andrés. I intend to ask King Datha the whereabouts of Cale, a city in La Florida where gold is even more plentiful, indeed, so plentiful that men wear helmets of the precious metal. I expect to find the glorious city of Apalache, reputed to be even more marvellous than Chicora and Cale. A very large, very rich metropolis. We are all fortunate: La Florida will make us rich and famous." Smiling, Don Pánfilo dismissed Vaca and Dorantes.

After thanking Vaca for having accompanied him, Dorantes went to his lodgings. "How different they are," he said to Esteban. "I do not think Narváez has learned anything. He wears his dead eye as proudly as if it was a medal from the king."

"Vaca and Narváez are like oil and water," Esteban said. "They will not mix."

Winter ended, and the spring. Month after month the sailing date was postponed, until His Majesty Charles V himself wrote to inquire pointedly when the conquest of La Florida would begin. It was the prod needed to get the expedition going. At last the time came when the members of the expedition quit their lodgings to settle themselves in their appointed places on the ships. Among the officers, the last to join, was another captain. Though his dress was modest, Dorantes noticed him immediately, for in addition to the regular luggage, he carried a lute.

Esteban missed the sight. He was watching some horses being carefully placed in their stalls below deck. A ticklish job, he thought, handling spirited animals who danced nervously at the hollow thud their hooves made on the gangplank. That afternoon while he and Dorantes were looking at the motley group of colonists climbing aboard —men with their wives, who were hoping to better themselves in La Florida—Dorantes mentioned the lute. "Not only shall we have tailors and bakers and candlestick makers to provide us with everything necessary to make life like home, we shall have music and song and dance. Perhaps we may teach King Datha to dance a pavan. Wait here. I see him. I want to meet the lute's owner."

Dorantes introduced himself, "Captain Andrés Dorantes de Carranca at your service." He noticed the other's sallow complexion that spoke of time spent indoors; at the same time it seemed to enhance his fine, sensitive features.

"And I am Captain Alonso Castillo de Maldonado, just graduated from the University of Salamanca." The voice was low, the manner quiet.

"Did I see you carrying a lute? Permit me to say, Don Alonso, that having music will make the whole voyage unexpectedly pleasant."

"Thank you for saying so," Castillo said. "I was afraid it would be thought out-of-place for me to bring my lute." And he smiled happily at Dorantes's attitude.

At last, on the seventeenth day of June in the year 1527, Pánfilo de Narváez, Governor of La Florida, richly attired in silk, flanked by friars and followed by his officials, officers, soldiers, and colonists led the parade from the church to the harbour, where small boats were waiting to ferry them. Trumpets sounded as he set foot on his ship. The spectacle satisfied him: Sanlúcar admired his fleet of five ships and his six hundred men.

The flotilla rode the high tide down to the ocean. As the sails filled with wind and as the land fell behind, the dreams and hopes and great expectations of the men were shadowed briefly by the possibility of disaster and death.

Sanlúcar de Barrameda, charged with glorious deeds, whispered of the high price paid for them. The town had witnessed the brave departure of the Admiral of the

Ocean Sea, Columbus himself, on his third voyage of discovery, from which he returned in chains, humiliated and bitter at royal ingratitude. And barely five years before their own sailing, the *Victoria*, battered and shabby, and her eighteen pitiful survivors had come home to Sanlúcar. Triumphantly hailed for being the first ship to circumnavigate the earth, it brought the tragic news that Magellan, the noble captain, had been killed by savages.

Now, as land faded from sight, each man knew a moment of panic. "Will I see my home again? my parents? my wife, my family? Will I return rich and noble, famous, successful? Will I return?"

Of them all, only Esteban already had his answer: he was alive, though Azamor and all it held for him was forever lost. His eagerness for the New World was not blunted by misgivings.

N OT EVEN WHEN they reached Santo Domingo, the first leg of the voyage, did anything happen to give an indication of the impending doom.

During the crossing, Dorantes and Castillo, young and of the same rank, became friends. For each it was a first experience away from home. Even their differences made their friendship richer. Where Dorantes was master of the sword and informed on what had been written about the New World, Castillo, son of a professor at Salamanca, had led a cloistered student's life. He had answers for all the questions his friend would throw at him.

"West: nothing to the northward, nothing to the south-ward." Every four hours as the watch changed they heard the helmsman sing out the course. During the long weeks this marked the passage of time.

"But at night, how do they know where west is?" Dorantes asked. And Castillo talked about the compass.

"A needle is magnetized. You understand? Good. For this the pilot has his lodestone. God has given such a needle a particular virtue—it is obliged to seek the north. To give the needle the necessary freedom to move, it is set on a pivot and the pivot sits in a circular bowl. Thus it can turn, as it must, to the north. From this it is simple to know all other directions."

Or Dorantes would delight in asking impossible questions—and there was always profit gained from Castillo's serious answers. Such talk made the days pass.

"What is an ocean?" Dorantes asked one day. "This *thing* Balboa discovered?"

"If you were my professor, I would answer thus: The ancients thought it was the Great River that encompasses the earth's disc. Whereas the learned Alcuin wrote in his *Grammar*: 'The ocean is the path of the daring, the frontier of land, the decider of continents, the hostelry of rivers, a refuge in peril, a treat in pleasure.' Since you are not my professor, I will say that you and I now know more about an ocean than the ancients and Alcuin."

Castillo told him about the debate that raged in the universities about the Indians of the New World: were they human? did they have souls? feelings?

At night when the air was warm, Castillo would sit on

the deck and play his lute. The men of the expedition listened to the sweet sound, enjoying the leisure and peace they knew would come to an end once they reached La Florida.

Gradually an uneasiness spread among the men. Narváez's overbearing arrogance bred doubts among the colonists and dissatisfaction among the soldiers—doubts and dissatisfactions that would come into the open as soon as they made port. Narváez's sense of self-importance led him to tell the captain of his ship which sail to hoist.

"He thinks his one eye is better than my two," the captain, outraged at being told his business, exploded to Dorantes. "Who does he think he is—the chief pilot of Spain? If he ever again tells *me* how to navigate I will remind him that at sea I give the orders."

Dorantes tried to calm him. "He is behaving as though he was already installed in his capital in La Florida."

"God grant that we may all live to see that," Castillo said. "At the university we were always reminded that pride goeth before destruction and a haughty spirit before a fall."

It was mid-September when the lookout gave the welcome cry: "Land! land!" The men crowded the rails to see. As the wind blew them quickly shoreward they saw the thin, dark line of land separating the immensity of the ocean from the immensity of the cloud banks grow thicker, greener, more solid, more distinct.

Esteban, who knew the look of the Atlantic coast of Morocco, marvelled at the unbroken green. Trees. Never had he seen such an expanse of trees, from the stands of mangroves that had their feet in the sheltered bays, across scrub growth that covered a flat plain, to soaring mountains on which the great giants rose, a forest so dense it crowded the valleys and hid the contours of the hills. Nothing moved but the wind, and in the sky, slowly circling hawks. Dorantes, glancing at Esteban's complete absorption in the tremendous view, could see in his eyes the awe he felt at the vastness, the lush richness, the beauty of the unspoiled land.

They had reached Santo Domingo; they would remain there for a month. Narváez, busy buying additional horses and provisions, did not seem to notice how men, colonists and soldiers, deserted the expedition by handfuls. One hundred and forty men, almost a quarter of his force, either because they were displeased with Narváez or because they had succumbed to the delights of Santo Domingo, stayed behind when the fleet sailed. Narváez seemed untouched by this—he forgot that desertions had prefaced his disaster with Cortés. He did not bother to ask why they had left, his only concern was to build up his force.

Next the fleet stopped at Santiago de Cuba where he was pleased to enlist replacements. Intent on keeping his expedition large and impressive, Narváez bought another ship, more arms, and horses. When a local resident offered to furnish additional provisions, he sent Vaca with two ships to that part of the coast nearest the resident's hacienda. He, with the four other ships, waited in the harbour of Santiago.

Until then, the New World had been generous and gentle.

A great storm swept down on that part of Cuba. Protected, the four ships rode it out. Days passed and Vaca failed to return. Narváez sailed his four ships along the coast, looking for the missing party. Nearing the place closest to the resident's hacienda, Dorantes and Castillo, in the lead ship, spied a handful of men. Boats were sent to bring them aboard. Vaca was the first to step onto the ship and was immediately closeted with Narváez so that he could report the tragedy that had overwhelmed the two ships.

Vaca tried to find a word to describe the force that had obliterated two stoutly built ships. He tried tempest, gale, wind—but none of them conveyed the proper sense of cosmic fury as well as the word the Indians of that region used for such a storm: "hurricane."

"Come to the point, Don Álvar Núñez," Narváez said.

"Your excellency ordered me to secure the provisions which had been offered. Our ships anchored offshore; there was no harbour, no protection. The hacienda was three miles inland. The sky was already dark grey; the wind was blowing hard; the sea was rough and troubled. The pilots urged me to fetch the provisions at once and get away as quickly as possible. They knew that part of the coast was an evil spot where many ships had foundered. Respecting their advice, I sent all the men ashore, hoping to speed the loading of the provisions.

"All of the men except thirty-two returned to the ships, miserable at having become drenched by the waves; they were wet, cold, and unwilling to go back to shore. Morning came. The sky was black, the sea ferocious. Twice a canoe braved the waves bringing word from the resident, urging me to come at once so that the provisions could be quickly put on board. The second time I went. Before leaving I told the pilots that if the south wind which they dreaded should blow, they were free to beach the ships and save the men and horses.

"Not a single man would go with me." Vaca stopped, overcome by the thought that to keep out of the drenching rain, the men had died by drowning. Narváez said nothing, nor did his face show any emotion. Vaca continued. "Hardly an hour after I left, the sea rose in a manner beyond belief. Then came the wind; the north wind blew with such power that the pilots were unable to drive the ships on the shore. More rain fell—a deluge poured down, so much for so long, without a letup.

"I had reached the men who were ashore; they were terrified. The wind lifted up huts and smashed them down. Still it increased in ferocity. To avoid being blown away, seven or eight of us would cling together. And so in terror and danger we wandered the whole night without finding a place where we could remain in safety for more than half an hour.

"Then came the most terrifying part: we heard a great noise after midnight, as though the door of Satan's hell had opened; we heard shouting voices, cries, and the sound of wild instruments—drums, trumpets, tambourines. With dawn the roaring ceased; the tempest passed. By all local opinions, your excellency, it was the worst such storm they had ever experienced."

"Pray come to the point, Don Álvar Núñez. My other ships may not have been inside of hell's cauldron, but we were on the rim and also felt its fury. There is no need for excuses. What happened to the ships? Where are the horses? Where is the rest of the party? You left with twenty horses, almost a hundred men, and two ships."

Unruffled by Narváez's callousness, Vaca continued his careful accounting. "I have given you a true account of what happened, not excuses. Early Monday morning, we who had stayed ashore hurried down to the sea. We saw no ships, only buoys floating on the water. We saw no sign of wreckage. We searched inland into the woods. After about a mile we beheld the little boat of one ship. It nested atop a tree where it had been blown. Later we combed the length of the beach and found the bodies of two men. I think they belonged to our party, but I could not be certain—they had been so smashed against the rocks their features were unrecognizable. A cloak, some box lids, a torn coverlet—nothing more. Of all, only the thirty-two men who went ashore the first day survived.

"We had days of hardship and hunger. In vain we tried to find the resident, but his hacienda was a pile of rubble; he was nowhere to be found. There is no need to tell you the enormity of the destruction the country-side suffered: crops washed out, cattle blown to their death, orchards and trees uprooted. A piteous landscape holding neither leaf nor grass."

Vaca had finished his report. When he came out of Narváez's cabin he found the men, having heard the survivors' accounts, standing stunned and frightened. The hurricane had flattened the courage of the soldiers. They demanded to spend the winter in the safety of harbour. They were permitted to return to Santiago de Cuba while Narváez, with his pilots and seamen, sailed to a nearby port to secure new ships to replace those lost.

A FEW WEEKS LATER Narváez rejoined his men; he had bought a ship and a brigantine.

"There seems to be no end to the money Don Pánfilo has to spend," Dorantes commented to Castillo.

"A brigantine is useful for landing parties in shallow water. But another ship! One he plans to leave behind with a squad of forty infantrymen and a dozen horsemen. A trifle extravagant, I agree. I am interested in the new pilot. Narváez seems all puffed up at having secured him. I wonder why?" Castillo asked.

When, a little bit later, Vaca joined them, he was preoccupied. "His excellency is congratulating himself on his new pilot. He has assured Narváez that he knows the exact location of the River of Palms. Not only that, he knows the entire coast of La Florida." Vaca's tone showed his scepticism.

"What do you think, Don Álvar Núñez?"

"I have never trusted men who claim to be experts in matters where nothing is known. The pilot sounds too accommodating—as though he knows Don Pánfilo's geography better than that of La Florida. In Estremadura the peasants would say 'the pilot is full of wind.' "

On February 20, 1528, the expedition started on the last leg to La Florida. Narváez had four hundred men—

the wives of the colonists stayed behind until they should be sent for—eighty horses, four ships, a brigantine, and complete trust in his new pilot. "Nobody can accuse me of carelessness," Narváez thought to himself. "I have secured an outstanding pilot who knows this coast as he knows the palm of his hand, and I have left a ship with reinforcements to be sent for if they are needed." He was very pleased with the arrangements he had made.

The ships sailed out of the harbour; their course was set to the northwest. The very next day, at sunset, the fleet piled up on one of the many shoals that abound in those waters. For fifteen days they were stuck there, the keels of their ships dangerously grazing the bottom. On March 8, a storm providentially lashed the waves high enough to float the ships. They continued on their course, Narváez's faith in his pilot untouched by this misadventure.

Not the pilot but a succession of violent March storms decided where along the coast that connects New Spain in the west with La Florida in the east—a lengthy, indented coastline that arches above the Gulf of Mexico—the expedition would first make land.

On Holy Thursday, April 14, the fleet anchored off the mouth of a bay. At last there was an end to the gales that had blown them first one way, then another. What should have taken seven days had taken seven weeks.

Far off, at the head of the bay they saw huts. A thrill ran through the men: this was the New World their king had given to them; here the golden cities of Cale and Apalache were waiting to be taken. They did not cheer nor dance. They were subdued by the silence and the immensity of the sight. The men watched anxiously as the first boat rowed toward an island in the bay; they watched until it returned safely. The advance party had obtained fish and pieces of venison by bartering glass beads and tiny bells.

"What does the know-it-all pilot say? Is this the mouth of the River of Palms?" Dorantes showered Castillo with questions, as though anyone who had been to a university should have the answers.

"Last night I saw the pilots using their cross-staffs. They seemed satisfied with our latitude," Castillo said. "The only question is whether we are east or west of the River of Palms, and by how much."

"Let them take measurements and find out."

"That, alas, is the crux of the problem. Latitude is easily reckoned. It tells us how far north of the equator we are. But longitude! Are we east or west of Santiago de Cuba? They can only guess; that is what dead reckoning is. To take an accurate reckoning for longitude they would need accurate hourglasses, astronomical tables, and much, much more mathematics than they have at their command."

"Castillo," Dorantes said, "are you telling me that the pilots know no more than we do? If this is true they are like players acting parts. For all their learned behaviour we are lost."

"When I dreamed of La Florida," Castillo added, "I took it for granted we would know where we landed. Our adventures were only to begin after that. I feel that the storms have most cruelly betrayed us."

"But Don Andrés—and you too Don Alonso—hasn't the whole enterprise always been filled with uncertainty?" Esteban asked the worried-looking young men. "Why are you here? Because you are ambitious, restless, curious, hopeful, anything—but not wise. Look at me: my father was wise when he bade me run for safety and here am I, too. If I understand Don Alonso, he is merely saying that the pilots are as lost as the rest. They say Pánuco is close by to the west; the friars claim it is to the east. Not one of them knows for sure. I think their arguments and play-acting are done to reassure themselves."

The next day, Good Friday, Narváez led a small troop to the *buhíos*, as in Santo Domingo they had learned to call the Indians' bark huts. They found them empty. During the night, without the whisper of a sound, the Indians had cleaned out their buhíos and stolen away in their canoes.

"Gold!" Suddenly the cry went up. A soldier poking among some fishnets had seen something glitter: a golden trinket. The Spaniards crowded around to look at it, to touch it. They laughed and shouted and danced and hugged one another as though drunk on a fierce brandy. Their wildest hopes had come true. If fishermen used gold, what treasures the king and nobles must have!

As was right, proper, and businesslike, the golden trinket was handed to the governor, who gave it to the chief assessor for safekeeping. In this manner they would deal with the riches of Apalache. The fishnet was torn to pieces, but like an evil charm, its golden trinket caught and held them.

HOW HAD IT ALL BEGUN? Where would it end? Spring and summer had passed; it was September 22 and the expedition, crowded into five homemade boats, was about to leave the Bay of Horses.

It began on April 16, when Pánfilo de Narváez took formal possession of the land: an impressive and auspicious beginning. His loud voice boomed out the proclamation of the royal grant and of his authority: the royal ensigns of Castile and Aragon were raised, and between them the friars erected a large cross. In the order of their rank, each of the various officials read his commission and had it acknowledged by the governor.

When this official act was completed, the expedition landed. Of all the horses purchased, only forty-two, lean and spent, survived the great storms and their protracted confinement. Some Indians appeared. From a distance they shouted words at the Spaniards, but without an interpreter they were not understood. There was, however, no misunderstanding their gestures: go away, go away, they motioned threateningly, but offered no violence.

The following day, the governor with his chief officials

led a small party northward to probe the land. By afternoon they reached another part of the vast bay that stretched far inland. They spent the night there and returned the next day.

Don Pánfilo was full of plans. He ordered the pilot in whom he placed such faith to take the brigantine and search for the harbour whose location he claimed he knew. If, he told the pilot, he failed to locate the River of Palms, he was to return to Cuba, take on provisions, fetch the boat that had been left behind and the two ships were to retrace the way back and look for the expedition.

"How credulous can you be? Only a fatuous man would still have faith in that know-it-all pilot," Dorantes mumbled. "First, he did not find what he said he could; second, he does not know where we are; and third, he cannot tell in which direction to look for the River of Palms."

"We'll never see him again. He is a smart man and knows when he's lost. I'll wager he heads straight for home," Castillo said.

The brigantine sailed away on her mission.

Narváez kept probing the land farther and farther to the north. A few days later his exploring party returned to the base. Dorantes and Castillo talked to Vaca who had been a member. "What did you find? What happened? Why is Don Pánfilo conferring so long with all the pilots? Are any plans made?" They bombarded him with questions.

"One question at a time," Vaca said. "I'll tell you what happened as it happened.

"As we were returning, we captured four Indians. We showed them some maize, for, as you know, maize is a sign of people who live in towns, perhaps in cities and kingdoms. Yes, those Indians recognized it and led us to a nearby village which we had not seen. Its fields were small and the maize not ripe for picking. But there we saw a most ugly, odious, strange sight. In each house we found a large bundle, in each bundle, a corpse. You know how merchandise is wrapped in Spain—just so were these bodies carefully wrapped in painted deerskins. Friar Juarez pronounced them idols and commanded us to burn them."

Castillo nodded. "He was right. There are witches still found in Spain who keep a coffin with a corpse that does their bidding."

"There might have been witches there too. But here our trail for gold began. In front of the bundles, among odds and ends of cloth and feathers, we found nuggets of gold. The assayer tested one. Questioning the Indians, we learned that these things are foreign to them. They told us by signs that they came from far away; we distinctly heard them say 'Apalache.' From what they indicated, Apalache has much gold and other things that are precious."

"How do you know that their signs mean what you think they do?" Castillo asked quietly.

"We don't," Vaca said frankly. He turned this thought over in his mind; it was disturbing.

"And then what happened?" Dorantes did not want to get sidetracked.

"We pushed on another thirty or forty miles behind our Indians who were guiding us to another town. It was small, only fifteen houses, but surrounded by large, well-tended gardens where the maize was ripe. We stayed there two days and then came straight back."

"If that is all, what are the pilots conferring about?"

"We told them where we went, what we saw, and everything we learned from the Indians so they could make a chart. Now Don Pánfilo is considering what we should do next."

Don Pánfilo called a council of his highest officials and presented his plan. His strategy was simple and direct: the expedition would forthwith establish its base at the mouth of the River of Palms. "Gentlemen," he said, "I suggest that the ships proceed along the coast until they come to the mouth of the River of Palms. The pilots are confident it is quite near. If they miss it they will reach Pánuco, our country's northernmost settlement on this coast. If necessary, we can secure new supplies there. While my ships sail there I will lead the men overland, through the interior, and effect a meeting." He smiled, pleased with his plan. With an unexpected modesty, he added, "If it please God, we shall capture Apalache on the way."

Aghast at the foolhardiness of the plan, Vaca reacted. He spoke slowly, marshalling his thoughts. "Your excellency, I will be brief. Under no circumstances should we leave the ships until we know where they are and that the harbour is safe. I have observed that the pilots do not agree as to our location—nor, in fact, do they know exactly where we are. I mean no offence to them when I say that they do not even know which part of La Florida we are in.

"Second, the horses are not yet fit to serve us in such emergencies as may arise. Lastly, but most important my lord, we have no interpreter. We cannot understand the natives, nor they us. How can we learn the truth about the country? I beg to remind you that we are about to enter a region of which no account exists. We are totally ignorant of its nature, its mountains, lakes, rivers—everything. We know nothing of its people. Do they, for instance, like some Indians, put poison on their arrows?

"Another consideration, different but equally important, is our food situation. We haven't enough to sustain us if we have to wander in search of—what? where? We can, perhaps, allow each man a pound of biscuit and a pound of bacon. Much too little to rely on in a country that, as far as we have seen, is poor—very poor.

"My lord, I urge you, be prudent as well as bold. Let us get away from here. Let us *all* embark again and find a good harbour and better country to conquer." Vaca finished his speech; urgently he pleaded for caution.

In vain. Of the officials present, only the notary sided with Vaca. The others were carried away by the words of Friar Juarez. "As our noble governor thinks of our bodily well-being, so I am concerned with our spiritual health." The friar spoke in a slow, honeyed tone. "The Almighty saved us from the fury of the storms—for what? He heard our prayers and protected us from the hurricane—for what? It is clear that we have been preserved for the glorious task ahead. We shall plant the Cross and bring salvation to unknown multitudes. It would be against the Will of God to embark again.

"I, for my part, am convinced that the pilots know that the River of Palms is a mere thirty or forty miles up along the coast. We cannot miss it. Don Pánfilo's concerted land and sea approach is inspired and bound to succeed. Let us not waste time. Forward to the mouth of the River of Palms. There, or else, Pánuco. By God's Grace we shall be reunited and ready for the conquest."

And so it was: caution was dismissed as cowardice. The governor's plan was put into operation immediately. The ships left, and on May 1 the march began.

Each man was allotted two pounds of biscuit and half a pound of bacon. No more, no less. Enough, Narváez figured, for the few days before they reached Pánuco. Three hundred men, of whom forty were mounted, started. Among those who rode was Friar Juarez, his four religious assistants, and the officers. The men trudged forward.

"How long can we get along on such poor rations?" Dorantes muttered while Esteban packed his gear. "Vaca explicitly said that the land is not rich and the buhíos few. When I see my cousin again I shall tell him about his One-Eyed One."

Castillo too left full of misgivings. "How can they say Pánuco is near? I have listened patiently to the pilots. They cannot even say how far west of Cuba we are. They dare not admit that the storms fouled all their reckonings."

For fifteen days the men marched; they met not a single Indian or village, house or garden. For fifteen days they straggled along, occasionally finding palmettos, whose innermost tender pith stilled their ever-mounting hunger.

They brought to the land strange new sounds—the clank of armour, the heavy thump of booted men, the murmur of Spanish curses, the whinnying of horses. And when the men, hungry and exhausted, stopped to sleep, they heard the land come alive with a hullabaloo of cries and roarings, howls, screechings, and shrill pulsating whistles. Just as the emptiness and silence of the day was ominous, so the wild noises of the night were fearsome and frightening.

At the end of the fifteen days they came to a river with a strong current. Exhausted by hunger and wearied by the long, hot march, it took a whole day to get the party across on crudely made rafts. On the other side of the river some two hundred Indians stood barring the way. Don Pánfilo went forward to meet them and started conversing by signs. Their answer was plain: threatening, mocking, insulting, they parodied him and laughed. "Further parley is useless," Narváez said. "Seize some of their leaders." Five or six men were grabbed; the others left without violence. The prisoners led the Spaniards to their village where in the gardens they found maize ready for picking.

"Let us give thanks to our Lord," said Friar Juarez. "He has saved us when we were in great and dire extremity." Willingly the men set up a cross and knelt in prayer. They fed well, they rested and were reassured. They were convinced that their sufferings were behind them and certain that the privations they endured would earn them the golden treasure of Apalache. They were ready to continue the quest. Unlike Ponce de León, who died from an arrow shot through his throat when he landed to claim La Florida for Spain, Narváez had not lost a single man on the march. "We are lucky," the men said.

They were still new to misery; worse was to come.

So far, indeed, they had been fortunate; the summer was just beginning. By its end they would count themselves lucky to escape alive from La Florida.

Still guided by the captured Indians, on May 17 they continued their journey. For a month they were led through ways in which only occasionally they caught a fleeting glimpse of an Indian—nothing more. This was the Indians' way of dealing with unwanted intruders.

And then, on June 17, a mighty chief, carried in state on the back of an Indian, came out to meet them. Dressed regally in painted deerskins, he was preceded by men playing flutes and surrounded by many attendants. Heartened by this first sight of regal splendour, Narváez announced by signs that he was on his way to Apalache. He understood the chief to say that the king of Apalache was his sworn enemy and that he would assist the Spaniards. With stately fanfare the chief led them back along the path to his village. It lay on the other side of a river, wide, deep, and with a rapid current.

They started the laborious task of ferrying men and horses—even with the help of the Indians' canoes, it went slowly. Impatient at the snail-like pace, one of the horsemen rode boldly into the river. The strong current swept him from his mount; he grabbed the reins, and both man and horse were drowned. Miles downstream the Indians found the dead horse and they, who had never before seen such an animal, stood looking at the strange beast. It provided supper for many of the Spaniards.

La Florida had claimed its first victim; gloom settled on the expedition. Their sadness lifted when, three days later, they entered the great chief's village. Maize was offered to them and they were invited to rest. A short-lived ease. That night a soldier was shot, and the Spaniards waited, alert for an attack to come. Nothing happened. When dawn came they found the village deserted. Warriors lurked all around the outskirts of the settlement but would not come when called to. By a ruse, three were captured and made to serve as guides.

The path the Indians took to Apalache led through a virgin forest whose giant trees were of a size the Spaniards had never before seen. Many were split from top to bottom where lightning had struck them. Many had fallen, creating obstacles that made progress tedious and strenuous. The heat grew more and more oppressive; the mosquitoes thicker; water was scarce and the Spaniards' hunger continued unappeased. But all ills were forgotten when, on June 24—almost one year to the day that the expedition had left Sanlúcar—they came in sight of Apalache. Through the trees they caught glimpses of the goal of their dreams and desires; the end of their sufferings.

Narváez ordered Vaca and the assessor to go ahead

with nine horsemen and fifty foot soldiers to make an entry into the city. Once inside they found only women and children, whom they herded together. Soon the warriors returned. There was a brief skirmish and the assessor's horse was killed by an arrow.

Everything was wrong, terribly wrong. The golden city consisted of about forty buhíos built low and scattered in sheltered spots against the hurricanes that lashed that region. Its golden treasure was yellow maize—an abundant amount ready for harvesting and much already gathered and stored. Around the town were not the rich mines they had imagined, but the same dense forest they had so laboriously penetrated. They also saw many lakes and ponds all cluttered with huge dead tree trunks. Any path they chose to leave by would be difficult and dangerous.

To stay was to be trapped. An uneasy truce was made. The chief of Apalache, who came to ask for the return of the women and children, was seized after Narváez had ordered them to be freed. He was kept as a hostage. When the warriors saw this, they attacked with fury and great cunning. They rushed in, set the buhíos afire, and fled instantly to the lakes where the Spaniards could not follow them. The expedition was ringed by hostile, elusive, and ever-watchful Indians.

Narváez questioned the captured chief about the region —its nature, its inhabitants, its cities. From him he learned that Apalache was by far the largest and richest settlement. To the north the land was poor and sparsely settled, and, still farther north, were large lakes, mighty forests, immense deserts and wasteland. To the south the country was better. Nine days march away was Aute, a town rich in garden produce. Being close to the sea the people of Aute also had fish.

Maize, beans, pumpkins, fish—this was the wealth of La Florida; otherwise it was a poor land, empty of cities and full of hostile Indians. The truth was too bitter to accept. Still hopeful, the Spaniards made forays in different directions. Everything they saw confirmed what the chief had said. Everywhere they went the Indians of Apalache gave them no peace. From behind trees and fallen logs, from fields of thick-standing maize, from safe hiding places, unseen, they sent their arrows. Many men and horses were wounded, for the best armour was no protection against arrows shot with deadly accuracy and power into unprotected parts of the body.

For twenty-five days the Spaniards stayed there. Then began the retreat.

Friar Juarez said it was a miracle that they escaped from the trap of Apalache. The Spaniards did not understand that the Indians wished nothing more than to rid themselves of intruders. That these, locust-like, had consumed their gardens was serious, but it was no cause for war. War was reserved for their enemies and was prepared for by the serious ritual of the war-party's drinking the Black Drink, singing sacred songs, and dancing. Those first Spaniards had not yet become official enemies. The Indians harassed them, prodding them out of their tribal territory; nothing more.

Indian harassment wounded many and killed a few,

but it kept the Spaniards moving at a fast pace and they reached Aute in nine days. The town was deserted; its houses burnt, but as the Apalache chief had promised, its gardens were laden with ripe produce. Here they rested and ate well for two days.

His arrogance and self-confidence dented, Narváez asked Vaca to find the way to the sea. With Friar Juarez, Captains Dorantes and Castillo, seven mounted men and fifty foot soldiers, Vaca set off.

During the day that Vaca's party was gone, Don Pánfilo and most of the others became violently ill. Greatly weakened by dysentery and wracked by agonizing cramps, the men somehow managed to stand off Indian attacks.

That evening Vaca's party returned, reporting that they had picked up a trail that brought them to salt water, the cove of a deep bay. There was a spring of sweet water, trees that shaded them from a burning sun, and an abundance of oysters on which the party had gorged.

"Your excellency," Vaca said when he saw the condition of the group, "let us leave a land so remote and malign. We are in a region so destitute of all resource that we can neither live in it nor get out of it. With God's help we shall escape."

Early in the morning of August 3, the expedition left Aute for the cove Vaca had reconnoitred. Now they had but a single thought—to get away from La Florida.

Landlubbers, they had cheerfully left their ships and pilots and seamen, and now, still landlubbers but without boats, without shipbuilding skills or any navigational experience, they faced a desperate sea voyage. Narváez's whole manner revealed that he knew he had failed completely. "The peacock has lost his tail feathers," Dorantes thought sadly. One third of his force was sick and the number increased hourly. Utterly beaten, Don Pánfilo wished it were possible to surrender to La Florida as long ago he had admitted his defeat to Cortés. What was left except to lay down and die? When he could see no other choice, he turned to his men for advice. They decided to take the one chance still open: to build boats and escape to Pánuco.

But the chastened, frightened governor declared it impossible. "We do not know how to make a boat. We have no tools, no iron, no forge. We have no oakum for caulking, no resin, and nothing with which to make the rigging. Even if we had everything necessary, we would not know how to put them together properly to fashion a boat. What will we live on while we work? Impossible!" he repeated shaking his head.

But the men, bred to the art of fighting, were determined to overcome their incompetence and engage in the useful arts of living. They thought and planned, considered and consulted with each other how to do the impossible.

In the camp, sick and wounded and well, officer and private were close together. There was no ease and little talk. Suddenly a soldier stood up and looked across to Don Pánfilo. He gave his name. "Pedro something-or-other," he mumbled, timid at addressing the governor. "Excellency, we need bellows to fan the fire. I have often watched the blacksmith in my village shaping iron. I have thought how to make such a contraption."

The men sat up straight, listening. "I could fashion the pipes out of wood and the bellows out of deerskins. Our stirrups, spurs, crossbows, and whatever else we have of iron will provide us with the nails, saw, axes, and whatever other tools we must have." Pedro sat down. There was a moment of silence after he finished as the men took the immense leap out of despair. Then all started talking at once—planning, suggesting, proposing schemes, volunteering for this or that task, remembering workmen's skills which as casual observers they had watched idly. Pedro's words, a call to battle for their own lives, stirred them; they were filled with courage, energy, and purpose. Of course they could escape. They would reach Pánuco. Everything became possible.

To transport themselves they figured they would have to build five boats, each thirty-eight feet long. They made measurements, drew plans, arranged schedules. Talents, unknown before, unused, were forthcoming. Besides the bellows-maker their experts included a carpenter and a Greek who knew how to obtain resin from pine trees. The others collected quantities of palmetto which they stripped of its fibres to make stuff for caulking; they plaited hair cut from the tails and manes of the horses into ropes and rigging; they sewed their shirts into sails. Their most difficult task was finding suitable stone to serve as ballast and anchors. No longer were they disappointed at not finding gold, now they cursed La Florida's scarcity of good, solid, heavy stone.

And food? How were they to feed themselves? They needed food for the workmen, the sick and wounded, and stores of food and water for the voyage ahead. For so considerable a provisioning they set up a schedule: each third day a horse was killed to supply good nourishment. Using whatever horses and men were fit, they raided the gardens of Aute—four armed forays gained them seven hundred bushels of maize. They also skinned the dead horses' legs entire and tanned them, thinking to provide themselves with leather water containers.

To keep the expedition alive while these preparations were being pushed, men went out at risk of their lives to collect shellfish in the nearby coves and creeks. In reprisal for the Spaniards' stealing their maize and beans, the Indians ambushed the small parties out collecting food. Twice they killed ten men in sight of the camp without their comrades being able to save them. Looking at their bodies being prepared for a Christian burial, Vaca remarked, "How precise and powerful is the natives' archery. Though our friends wore their best armour, arrows have gone clear through their bodies. May God have mercy on us."

They worked hard. After forty-seven days, on September 20, the boats were finished and so was the provisioning for the voyage. Forty men had died of starvation and twenty more had been killed by the Indians. This reduction in number permitted the living to take small bundles of clothes. The men were assigned their places. Boat One, commanded by Narváez, carried forty-nine men—he had selected the healthiest and most able; Boat Two, commanded by Friar Juarez and the notary, had the same number; Boat Three, with forty-eight men, was commanded by Captains Dorantes and Castillo; Boat Four, with forty-seven men, was commanded by the other two captains, Peñalosa and Tellez; and Boat Five, with forty-nine men, was commanded by Vaca and the assessor.

They had a rehearsal to see if everything was in order, and when the men, provisions, and scant supplies were stowed away, the boats rode so low that the sides cleared the water by half a foot. The men, tightly packed together, could barely move. Though cramped and crowded, weighed down and fearful of storms and turbulent seas, they were ready. Magnificently, heroically, out of nothing they had created a means of escape.

Mass was said; the friars heard confession. The last horse was killed and eaten. The boats pushed off. The place they left they called the Bay of Horses.

FOR A WEEK the boats probed the shores of the vast indented bay seeking an opening to the sea and Pánuco.

"If I had my choice," Castillo said jokingly, though the sharp edge of his worry showed, "I would invite my professor of astronomy to join us rather than my sainted professor of theology. All of us can hope to reach heaven —we know what to do and what not to do. But how can we hope to find Pánuco without there being a single navigator in the entire party?"

"But as surely as night follows day we shall know

where the west is," Dorantes said. Then he understood the full meaning of Castillo's words and added, "How will we find our way in fog or rain? and at night? And when winds and currents carry us whither they will?"

"Ah, then we must rely on Divine guidance."

Where? How could it end? These were questions they dared not ask aloud.

It did not take them long to discover that they had exchanged one kind of hell for another. The next weeks were crucial. When, soon, the water containers made from the horses' legs began to rot, thirst haunted them as well as hunger. They were forced to put in to land to get drinking water. Sometimes in the night they would hear Indians, but they did not see or meet any. One morning they rowed to an island hoping to find water without risking an encounter with natives. The island, a spit of sand, had none. As the boats lay at anchor, a sudden tempest engulfed them, making a dark fury out of sky and sea. Unable to brave the waves, the men stayed on the island for six terrible days while the thirst which had sent them there remained unquenched. Four men went crazy and greedily drank salt water. That same night they went into convulsions and died.

The storm was less terrifying than the lack of water. Their comrades' deaths decided them. Rather than wait to perish from their intolerable thirst they would risk the perils of the waves. They embarked. The boats proved staunch, and by sunset they doubled a point of land and found shelter with much calm.

Indians came out in canoes; tall and well-built, they

carried no bows and arrows. Because of this and to satisfy their thirst, the men headed their boats for the beach where the buhíos were. Before each house were many clay pitchers filled with water and pots filled with cooked fish. The village chief ceremoniously brought Narváez to his house and presented him with fish. In return, the Spaniards offered maize which the Indians ate. Everything was amiable. The governor was delighted to be asked to spend the night there. All were comfortably lodged except the sick who, too weak to walk, stayed on the shore.

At midnight, by a prearranged signal, the Indians suddenly fell on those in the buhíos. Not bows and arrows fired from a distance, but great stone maces which they wielded with ferocious skill were their favourite weapons. Narváez, his face smashed in, was led to his boat for safety, while some fifty Spaniards held back the Indians. After a second attack had been repulsed, the four captains with some dozen soldiers hid, and when a third wave came on, fell on the rear of the attackers. The Indians fled; the Spaniards gathered together to see what losses they had suffered. Hardly a man had not been touched by the maces, and three of the sick lying on the shore had been killed. They grabbed the earthen water pitchers and pushed out to sea.

October was ending; cold, sudden and severe, increased their misery.

When the little water they had was exhausted, they again put in to shore. The new region they came to was richer. The chiefs had long, flowing hair which added greatly to their handsome appearance, and were wrapped in richly worked blankets of marten skins; they carried themselves proudly. Here, again, the chiefs first feigned friendship and then attacked; again they used the head-crushing war clubs. When the Spaniards retreated to their boats, they were showered with stones sent stinging from slingshots. The Indians attempted to block their escape by closing the little harbour with warrior-filled canoes. A freshening breeze filled the sails, and with the rowers pulling hard, the Spaniards forced their way out and left the Indians behind.

On they went, following the coast to the west. Until then they had suffered hunger—men had died of starvation, and those who lived and worked, fought and rowed did so on a daily ration of a handful of maize chewed grain by grain; they had suffered grave, prolonged thirst —and men had died of it; they had fought off Indian attacks, each time leaving a few dead behind. But all these weeks they had been together. Being united had given them reassurance as well as strength.

For all their desperate ignorance of seamanship and navigation, they had made progress toward Pánuco. By following the coast, inevitably, unexpectedly they came to where the mightest river in North America sends its waters into the sea. Who was there to warn them? They were the first Europeans to see that giant river push the sea back, maintaining its riverine freshness far from land.

There, at the mouth of the river the Indians called Mississippi, on the first day of November, the boats separated; the expedition fell to pieces. Why? why? Many

times the survivors asked the question. In part it was Narváez's incompetence—but that was an old story—and his arrogance, which misfortune had soured into selfishness. In part it was their helplessness before the forces of river and tempest and sea. So invincible was the river's current that even using all their muscle could not gain them the land; they felt it far out at sea and found the muddy water sweet and potable. A fierce icy wind blew from the north driving them, through the night, still farther offshore.

When morning came the boats had lost sight of one another, but by afternoon, wind and current brought three fairly close together. The governor in Boat One hailed the nearer of the two boats. It was Boat Five with Vaca.

"Vaca is that you?" Narváez shouted through cupped hands.

"Yes, excellency."

"What would you advise? Our getting separated—" a gust of wind blew away his booming voice.

"Let us row with the current and join the boat ahead. We must stay together. Until Pánuco—stay together." Vaca spoke slowly; the last word floated over the water lengthened, prolonged.

"They are too far out. I intend going ashore."

"But excellency," Vaca began to remonstrate, but Narváez kept on shouting.

"Follow me, Vaca—can you hear?—if you wish to stay with me. Tell your men to take their oars and work.

Work hard. My men are putting all their strength into rowing."

"Don Pánfilo," Vaca shouted, unable to believe what he heard. "It will take all our energy. Must we?"

"If we do not get to land now we shall be blown out to sea and starve to death." As Narváez said this his men began to pull hard. His word was still law; obediently Vaca and his men rowed to catch up. Hard and desperately they pulled at the oars, but as the sun started setting Vaca saw they would not be able to keep up with Narváez's boat, powered by the strongest and healthiest. Just before Narváez pulled farther ahead, Vaca shouted, "Throw us a line. Light is fading. Then we'll be able to stay together."

"You did not work hard enough," came the cold answer.

"Don Pánfilo, we have obeyed you as we took our oath to do. We have done our best, but our best is not good enough to catch up with you. What shall I do?"

"Lord Treasurer," the use of the title had an official sound, "the time has come when I cannot command you or any other officer. Each of you is empowered to do what seems best to save himself. I shall act in this way; you do likewise."·

With these words the two boats separated. Vaca would never see Narváez again. He ordered his men to row with the current to join the other boat drifting away from the land. It waited. For a few days Boats Four and Five kept each other company, alone on the open sea. Then a storm blew them apart.

Vaca's boat rode out the storm. At sunset of the second day, hunger, severe buffeting from the waves, and thirst created a deep despair. Barely moving, half-conscious, the men lay huddled in groups to keep warm; only Vaca and another had strength enough to steer through the night. In the cold light before dawn, Vaca heard the sound of breakers. Pulling as hard as he could on the land side of the boat, he kept a distance from the surf.

Without warning a mighty wave suddenly seized the boat and raced it toward the shore. The shock with which it hit the sand roused the men to consciousness. They crawled ashore. In a ravine they found protection from the fresh, cold wind. They made a fire, parched some maize, found a pool holding rainwater, and responding to the warmth and food and solid ground, revived bit by bit.

When the sun came out, things looked brighter. Vaca told Lope de Oviedo, a brave soldier and the strongest of the group, to climb a nearby tree and see what he could see.

"We are on an island, sir." After looking carefully, he said with great excitement, "God be praised. A Christian country. The ground is pawed up as on a cattle range."

"Can you see any roads?"

"Perhaps a footpath."

Vaca bade him climb down and follow the path a little way to see where it led. After some time, Lope returned with an earthen pot, a little dog, a few mullets, and—

beckoning them on while they lagged behind calling out to him—three Indians armed with bows and arrows. Others soon joined the trio until there were a hundred armed warriors; tall, sturdy, they looked gigantic to the exhausted, defenceless Spaniards huddled in their protected ravine.

Calmly and with great dignity Vaca approached them, bearing such gifts as he still had—some beads and tiny, tinkling hawkbells. They presented him with an arrow, a sign of friendship. By signs they promised to return with food. This meeting came at a most fortunate moment. The Capoques and Han tribes were enjoying their short season of plenty. Their weirs yielded a supply of fish and their staple—the new roots of a kind of cattail that grew in the tidal flats—was just then in abundance. Twice the next day they brought food for the men.

The generosity of the Indians enabled the men to accumulate a supply of fish and edible roots. After some days they felt sufficiently rested and restored to want to continue their quest for Pánuco. The friendliness of the Indians had nourished their hopes as well. They took it as a happy omen that the worst was behind them and soon they would be home among their countrymen in New Spain.

With great effort they dug their boat out of the sand which had half-buried it. They stripped to keep their clothes dry while launching the boat in the surf. The water was surprisingly warm, but the task took all the strength they could summon. They climbed in, weak, awkward. Two waves in rapid succession caught the boat and capsized it. Three men clinging to its upturned bot-

tom were drowned; the rest, pulled along by a foaming wave, were thrown on the beach, vomiting the seawater they had gulped.

Wet and naked—everything gone—they would have perished if they had not found a few live sparks in the fires they had left. They looked at their bodies—skin-covered skeletons. While warming themselves they wept for their comrades who had perished and their own terrible predicament.

At sunset, the Indians returned. Alarmed by the change, they drew back. Vaca called to them and went forward, naked Spaniard meeting naked savage. By signs he explained what had happened, showing them two of their dead comrades whose bodies had been washed ashore. And when, finally, the Indians understood, they lamented loud and long.

Their grief moved Vaca. Turning to Lope, he said "How strange to see these wild, untaught men howl over *our* misfortunes. Hearing them, I feel our calamity the more." By signs he managed to ask the Indians to take the Spaniards into their buhíos.

They had their first lesson in how naked savages keep alive when going distances in freezing weather: the Indians built great fires at intervals, and half-carrying those too weak or cold to run, rushed them from bonfire to bonfire. The buhíos they had prepared were also warm and bright with the many fires they had lighted. Rejoicing at the rescue they had performed, the Indians sang and danced all night. Again they brought fish and roots. In the face of such good treatment and hospitality, the

Spaniards ceased fearing that they had been saved only to be sacrificed in some diabolic rite to a heathen idol.

A few days later Vaca happily welcomed Dorantes, Castillo, Esteban and all their men. The men of Boat Three were shocked at the plight of Vaca's party; and sad, too, that they had nothing to share with them. They had only the clothes they wore.

Later Castillo related the end of their boat journey. "Don Álvar Núñez, the same current that carried you, brought us. We thought we were in good shape, when our boat capsized in a rip current on the other end of this island. We met some Indians. Esteban says they call themselves the Han. They brought us food and treated us well. We spent our days trying to repair the boat, using driftwood. Despite all our efforts, when we put her in the water, she sank. We could not make her seaworthy. We have decided to continue along the coast until, with God's help, we reach the land of Christians."

"No, Castillo. The weather is bad. What will you do when you come to rivers and bays? How will your men swim across? They are too weak. I suggest that the four most robust men who are strong swimmers push on to Pánuco. It cannot be far. They can sound the alarm and summon help. It is better to stay here for the winter. There is food for all." Vaca felt it was better for the parties to stay together.

So four men started out on their mission. Some place, somehow, they perished along the way, for no alarm for the survivors was ever given.

Soon, very soon, the season of plenty the Capoques

and Han were enjoying, ended. No longer did fish swarm into their weirs; the roots on which they had lived for two months were old, tough, inedible. The Indians had nothing to give the Spaniards, and the Spaniards had no knowledge of how to live in so barren a place. As the men starved and died, they called their refuge the Island of Misfortune.

Of the eighty men who reached there in November, by April only fourteen would remain alive.

3 / The Walk

SOMETHING OUT OF THE ORDINARY brought the Indian to the buhío shared by Vaca, the brave soldier Lope, Castillo, Dorantes, and Esteban. The Indian said something, and Esteban, the first to speak words in the Capoques' language, listened attentively. He wanted to be certain he understood. Hunger had settled on the island for the Indians as well as the Spaniards.

"There is sickness in his family," Esteban told Vaca. "They want us to heal."

"What did you answer?" Vaca asked the question for the others. His qualities won him the respect his position as commander entitled him to. "Are you sure you understood?"

"Quite. He spoke of trouble, and I was not sure whether he meant inside the group or inside a man. That is why he pointed to his stomach when I asked," Esteban explained.

"It is impossible," Dorantes said flatly. "What if the person dies? It will be our fault."

"How can we act as physicians? We have never taken examinations, we have no diplomas." For Castillo that settled the matter; he looked surprised when the others laughed.

"We could claim we lost our credentials with our clothes," Vaca said with a straight face. "Seriously," he continued, after Castillo joined in the laughter, "what Dorantes says is true. Of course, we could be killed if we fail. That is a risk even a proper physician takes. I do not mind pretending. But what if we succeed? We may risk our salvation. Success might be Satan's way of tempting us."

"Don Álvar Núñez," Esteban said, "one further thing the Indian said before he left. They will not bring us any more food until we do as they ask."

"Ah, I smell Satan!" Castillo said. "This is a moral problem. Shall we imperil our souls for the comfort of our bellies?"

And they were silent as they contemplated having hell everlasting after enduring so much on earth. They had seen an Indian healing ceremony, watched the medicine man perform his rites by blowing on the patient's body and laying on his hands.

"The medicine man did devilish things," Dorantes said, "when he claimed he drove out an evil spirit lodged in the man's chest."

"I feel as Don Álvar Núñez does. It is a heathen practice and should not be countenanced by Christians." Castillo voiced his opinion. Lope nodded solemnly in agreement.

Vaca looked from one to the other. "And you, Esteban?" he asked. "What do you think? You have told us what the Indian said, but not what you think. We are in this together. Every man's opinion is important."

Esteban began slowly and spoke seriously. "You scoff

at them. Laugh. Pass judgment. You Andrés, you know I am a Christian. I know myself as one who believes deeply and truly. But I also remember what my mother believed. My father believed in Allah—but my mother! Often when I was sick she burned certain leaves and let the smoke bathe me. She did as she had seen her people's priests and diviners do to expel the evil spirits who brought pain and misfortune. She had never been taught the True Faith; she spoke of an All-Wise Creator to whom her people prayed for health and good fortune. Because of this I do not feel that trying to heal an Indian would harm either him or us."

They listened to him, but his words did not change their minds. Stolidly they refused to try to cure the sick man. Two days passed without any Indian coming to visit them. Then their first friend, the Indian who had given Vaca the arrow, came with the same request. He spoke emphatically and was silent as, phrase for phrase, Esteban translated.

"He says," Esteban said, listening carefully, "he says: You are unwise. Believe what I tell you. We know certain stones and pebbles have power. Great, good power. When such stones are passed over the sickness, their power removes the pain and restores good health. Like such stones or pebbles, you are extraordinary. Different from other men; men on this island; men along the mainland. You have white skin and black skin, not like other men. This must mean that you have power. Greater than the pebbles. Use it. Help us." And when he had finished he left.

"Do you still feel the same?" Vaca asked.

Castillo was the first to speak. "I have been thinking. Maybe hunger has cleared my mind. Or maybe from what Esteban said I begin to understand why they demand this of us. Like him, I too have been remembering. Once when many students were ill, the rector of the university invited an astrologer to find the cause. He did not consult pebbles; he studied the stars and announced that the illness lay in certain planets. He assured us that the signs were auspicious and all would change in two weeks. We got well. Was it, I have been wondering, because we believed what he predicted?"

"Faith is a great force," Vaca said. "In Estremadura they say faith in the physician is half the cure."

"I too have been thinking about our danger," Esteban said. "And it seems to me that whatever sin there is in pagan practices, there is no blasphemy in the prayers we offer and the blessing we ask."

"If God is merciful and their faith in us is strong, perhaps we shall help them," Vaca said. "Let us go to the sick man."

The man lay moaning, his troubled eyes looked wildly from side to side. They kneeled around him, breathed on him, recited an Our Father and a Hail Mary; then they prayed silently, fervently. They finished the ceremony by making a large sign of the cross over him. Hardly had they finished when the patient got up, calmed and eased, announcing that his pain was cured.

For bringing one of their number back to health, the

Indians treated them well, sometimes denying themselves food that they might give most of the little they had to the Spaniards. Even with such eager goodwill, there were times when for two or three days nobody had anything to eat.

Driftwood was plentiful and enabled them to enjoy the warmth of bonfires. February had almost ended. For two days it had stormed and for two days they had tasted no food.

Vaca said to the group huddled around the fire, "Nothing I have read, nothing I have seen or could have imagined would have prepared me for the wretched, uncertain life these people lead. I have seen hungry peasants; I have seen people left without food in a place where armies fought; I have heard of famines when crops fail. But such are disasters—temporary. They are not a permanent condition. For the Capoques, however, hunger is the very condition of life."

"How unfortunate they are compared to those of La Florida," Dorantes added. "Now I can appreciate the storehouses of Apalache and the gardens of Aute. Agriculture gave those Indians, whose poverty we despised, both safety and ease. Here they are always on the ragged edge of starvation."

"My thoughts," Castillo said, "are less generous. Sometimes I have likened the Capoques to animals—like sheep who graze all the time, or like wolves who are forever prowling, or even like bears who hibernate during the winter. These men and women spend all their time and all their strength looking to find enough just to keep alive. And yet they are not animals. They have deep human emotions. I have never seen people who love children—all children—more."

Vaca agreed. "They are still mourning a boy who died months before we came. His family weeps and cannot be consoled, and the whole group weeps with them."

"Three times a day," Dorantes said, "morning, noon, and night. That is the wailing we hear."

"That was for a son. A child is something precious and special," Vaca said. "They seemed quite indifferent when that old man died."

"They remarked that his season was passed and he had no enjoyment," Esteban explained. "They complained about the food the old man ate; much better to have fed the children. That is their logic."

"The harshness of their existence gives such logic validity," Castillo said.

"My friends," Vaca said after a pause, "listening to you has made certain ideas begin to take shape. We sit here and talk, comparing the Capoques to animals, and in the very next breath admiring their intense love of children. They have nothing of value, not even clothes; they are ignorant, stupid, savage. Nevertheless, they live and cherish one another, sing and dance, are merry. We are still alive because the Indians shared their pittance with us. I am torn between pity for the terrible poverty of their lives and a deep admiration for their knowledge of how to survive in so unlikely a region."

"Don Álvar Núñez, our professors could not have stated the matter better. I keep remembering our learned discussions about the nature of the Indians of the New World," Castillo said. "We never even considered that there might be people who existed without animals or crops. All those definitions of what a human being is—" Castillo waved them away. "Now I would state unequivocally: To be human is to be generous. These are human beings. The greater because they have so little."

Naked as the savages they were discussing, they looked at one another. Again it was Vaca who, putting his thoughts into words, gave them a goal to work for. "We shall do well to learn from them how to exist in such poverty and uncertainty. Only thus and with God's help shall we not suffer the fate of our comrades. Despair, as well as starvation and cold, can kill. We must survive and live to find our way to Pánuco."

"Amen, amen," Dorantes said.

"Don Álvar Núñez, you are right. If we learn the ways of the savage we can conquer the wilderness in which they live. What a bizarre university this is," Castillo said. "As one student to another in the same class, I hail Esteban who has outdistanced us all—he can already speak with the Capoques. How do you do it?"

"Perhaps my advantage is that I had a little of the savage in me to begin with," Esteban said, smiling. "Remember, it was not so long ago when I was forced to learn Castilian. I had to listen close and hard. Your words and sounds—they were different from the tongue the Portuguese spoke. A fifth language comes easier than the second one. You will see. I find the best way is to try to imitate—that is good for the tongue and the ears. Alonso, I guarantee that before we reach Pánuco we will meet many people speaking many different languages. Did you notice that the Han who are just on the other side of this island speak a different tongue?"

"The Han have other differences," Dorantes said. "They are not so completely naked as the Capoques. Their men wear a long narrow reed passed through a slit made from side to side of one or both of their nipples. They also insert a small reed through their underlip."

"Must we decorate ourselves likewise, Don Álvar Núñez, when we learn to live like savages?" Lope de Oviedo asked. The good soldier was a little confused as to what was expected of him.

"No, Lope," Vaca answered. "It is learning the essentials of how to survive, not their fashions, that we must copy."

So, out of utter necessity, but with the full force of a purpose and a driving hope they began a long, bitter, desperate schooling in the art of survival.

The year 1529 was beginning.

FOR THE CAPOQUES, the year was divided by the foods which became available in the different parts of their territory. From October to March they put up their reed buhíos on the Island of Misfortune, catching fish in weirs. But this was a chancy pursuit: only during November and December could they rely on a plenty of cattail roots dug from the tidal flats. It was by incessant toil that the women secured a bountiful supply. Harvesting the roots left the ground pitted—the sight Lope de Oviedo had mistaken for meadows churned by cattle. When, in January, the cattails started growing and their roots became inedible, hunger stalked the group.

Hunger became more acute whenever a son or brother died; then members of the stricken household would sit and mourn for three months. In all that time they depended on food supplied by relatives and friends. In the winter, when many died, hunger was great in most houses. Feeding so many mourners taxed the meagre supplies the others collected.

One evening in late March, Esteban entered the buhío; the last to come in, he was out of breath from hard running. He had been detained by the Indians. He brought bad news: they were to be separated. Vaca and Lope, the two who had first made contact with the Capoques, were to go to the mainland with the family of the man who had presented Vaca with an arrow in token of friendship.

"How long will we stay?" Vaca asked, disturbed at their being parted.

"It is hard to say, Don Álvar Núñez," Esteban answered. "As long as they find an abundance of oysters in the bays. That is what I understood. After that they go to another place to live on blackberries. Other groups come there for the same food. This they enjoy, for there will be much singing and dancing."

"Then we must figure on an oyster season and a blackberry season before we are reunited." Vaca was trying hard to plan ahead. "And the others?"

"Those who were in your boat will go with other Capoques. We—" and Esteban indicated Castillo, Dorantes, and himself, "we are to go back to the Han. They received us first. That's how they're distributing us."

"Are the Han among the groups that go to the blackberry patch?" Vaca asked, deeply concerned.

"I did not ask. We can only hope so," Esteban answered.

"I had not counted on our being separated. It doesn't look good." It was Vaca who broke the silence that held them. "We must accommodate ourselves to them. We cannot live without them." He stood up. "Come, Lope. Having nothing, we are quite ready. How simple it is to move with no clothes to pack, no gear to put in order." He looked intently at the three he was leaving. "I shall never, never give up trying to regain our fellowship. As long as I live, and with God's help and mercy, I shall look for you. Somehow we shall be reunited and together continue our quest for Pánuco. Come, Lope." And so Vaca and Lope went with the Capoques. With the others from their boat they went across to the mainland.

Cast out by the Capoques, Castillo, Dorantes, and Esteban returned to the Han and prevailed on them to receive them as slaves. In their canoes they crossed to their part of the mainland, glad to have escaped from the island. They did their best, toiling alongside the women, collecting firewood, which here was scarce, and oysters, which were plentiful. The water, brackish and smelling of marsh gas, nauseated them, and hordes of mosquitoes tormented them. But their miseries were forgotten when, without warning, their masters set them free.

One who spoke the language of the Capoques told Esteban of the decision.

"Andrés! Alonso!" Esteban joined them where they were picking blackberries, their clothes torn and shredded by the sharp brambles. "They are returning to the island without us."

"What did they say?" Dorantes asked.

"How can they abandon us?" Castillo asked at the same moment.

"He told me, 'Find new masters. You do not do enough to feed yourselves. We are weary of keeping you. Go away. Find new masters. There are some Indians in another bay—two days' walk there. Go to them.'"

The three looked at one another, stunned. Castillo was the first to handle the terror that gripped them. He said lightly, "We have been expelled from the Han university. I am glad I had not begun the study of their language."

"We must peddle our wares elsewhere," Esteban said, looking at their scarecrow figures. "At least we shall not be far from the Capoques and Don Álvar Núñez will be able to follow us."

"We had better take the advice and seek the tribe he mentioned," Dorantes said. "And pray that they are willing to receive us. We will need them to show us where the oyster beds are and whatever else they eat."

To quiet the fears that filled them, they took an oath never to stop, even if death stood in the path, until they came to the country of the Christians. Having sworn, they shook hands solemnly. The oath and handshake gave them reassurance, joining the three in a private ritual of great meaning: henceforth they were friends, equal in their struggle and determination. "We shall renew our oath when we are reunited with Vaca, Lope, and the others," Dorantes said, expressing their common hope.

They had need of all the courage and stamina they could summon.

The Indians they met lived solely on fish and moved frequently. From them the three learned how brutally a slave can be treated and how defenceless he is. The Indians robbed them of their few rags, punched them, beat them with sticks spiked with thorns, and to amuse themselves, tugged at the Spaniards' beards—they could not believe that men grew hair on their faces.

How different these Indians, who called themselves Mariames, were from the Capoques and Han. Cross-eyed, crabbed, and cantankerous, suspicious and superstitious, they quarrelled frequently and killed easily. When they fought they used their fingernails, grown long and kept sharp, to slash and cut—they reminded the Spaniards of spurs on fighting cocks.

When spring came again, Castillo was the first to press for change. "Privation and continual labour can be endured. But the Mariames have no redeeming qualities. Let's leave them. Our new masters—no matter who—cannot be more—" he hunted for the word to use and came out with the mild "disagreeable."

"Vicious would be a better word," Esteban said.

"How will we get across the bay?" Dorantes asked. "The Mariames control this side and will track us if we try to walk around."

"We could try to get to the Ygauzes," Esteban suggested. "The Mariames call them witches and demons—that is one way of seeing your enemies. The point is they will not dare to follow us into Yguazes territory."

"Right," Castillo said. "Let's try the Yguazes. Frankly, I have had enough fish. Let's try the fare of an inland group."

Escape was easy. Either the Mariames were glad to be rid of three extra mouths to feed or they no longer suspected them of wanting to run away and did not watch them closely. While out collecting firewood, they made their way to the first line of hills where the territory of the Yguazes commenced.

Quite soon they knew that as intruders they were being watched. There was no going back; they went forward, walking steadily. Suddenly half a dozen men stood across their path. The three showed that they had no weapons. They avoided using the language of the Mariames for fear they would be taken as allies of the enemy. By signs they asked to be accepted as slaves, prostrating themselves before the Indians. Led to the encampment, each found a master.

They had succeeded; they were especially pleased that the Yguazes had accepted all three.

Their territory, dry and desolate, did not support large game. Occasionally, the men, who were excellent archers, would shoot a deer or fish, but for the most part the group relied on what the women collected—spiders,

grasshoppers, snakes, lizards, grubs and ant-eggs, rotted wood and the dung of deer. And roots. When everything else failed, there were roots. Difficult to dig out of the hard ground, they were also difficult to make edible. Even after being roasted for two days they had a bitter taste and could cause severe cramps. But the roots kept them alive until the happy season of the prickly pear.

Sometimes the four accompanied their masters on a deer hunt. From them they learned how to run from morning until night pursuing a deer until it tired or until they could overtake it and kill it with an arrow.

Why? Andrés, Alonso, and Esteban often asked each other in the long time they spent with the Yguazes, why did they stay? They knew the Indians to be thieves—but that did not worry them since they possessed nothing. They knew them to be liars—or was it that the truth was so impossible that they dismissed it as a lie? They knew them to be great drunkards, getting sodden on a drink they concocted from the cactus peyote. In spite of all this and the hunger that haunted them, the Yguazes were a merry people who loved to dance and keep whatever festival they had reason to celebrate. "Happy, happy," were the words they spoke often and with gusto.

"I know what happiness looks like," Esteban said, holding a prickly pear in his hand. "It is the size of a hen's egg and vermilion and black in colour."

"I know what happiness tastes like," Dorantes said. "Most agreeable in flavour and as much as the appetite wants."

"I know all this and I also know what happiness is," Castillo said as the three lolled, surrounded by food within easy reach. The Yguazes were camped where the prickly pear grew in abundance, having made the long journey as soon as the season had come. They lay at ease.

"I thought they were lying when, after we had gone without food for a few days, the women would smile and say, 'happy, happy prickly pear.' We still had four or five months to wait," Esteban said. "They were trying to give us courage by talking of the feasting to come." He stretched himself lazily.

"And themselves, too," Dorantes said. He belched. "Excuse me."

"A belch that comes from a full stomach is a fine sound," Castillo said. "I will confess," he continued, "that I thought Esteban was making it all up when he translated what the women said. He was right; they were right: 'Happy, happy. The bellies will be full and the lovely juice will run over and down on the chest.' " He sighed with contentment.

But the prickly pear region also had clouds of mosquitoes, a torment that ruined the pleasure.

"I have studied the mosquitoes," Castillo said. "They are of three kinds."

"I have studied them too." Dorantes took up the talk. "There are three kinds, but they poison and inflame equally. Don't they bite you?" he asked Esteban.

"I wish they did not, Andrés. I have studied the mosquitoes and find that to them blood is blood no matter what the colour of the skin. It's just that my skin does not show the bites as clearly. I am glad I do not look as though I had a bad case of the pox."

The Yguazes protected themselves from the pests by circling their buhíos with fires made of wet, rotten wood to produce smoke without much flame. The smoke choked the three and they sought the beach where the breeze kept the mosquitoes away; but their masters would wake them up with blows and order them back to the encampment to keep the fires going. In spite of the discomforts and indignities, Castillo, Dorantes, and Esteban enjoyed the plenty and ease of the prickly pear season.

Every other year, when the prickly pear season ended, theYguazes travelled far inland to camp in a grove of fine pecan trees, where for two months they would stay eating the rich, tasty nuts. They were sad only that the trees did not bear a big harvest every year; late summer and early fall were the happy, happy months of carefree eating.

Thus between starvation and satiety, season followed season. The years passed. They were alive, toughened and adept in the ways of surviving. They had learned to be patient.

"Impatience ill-becomes the weak," Castillo said when Dorantes complained of the slow passage of time.

"Impatience is the privilege of the free. I learned patience and hope when I became a slave," Esteban said. "One day I—we—shall be free. The only questions are how and when."

"And also," said Dorantes, "how long should we wait for Vaca and Lope?"

Often, but always in an off-hand manner they talked of leaving, of starting for Pánuco. Yet they knew that to fret, to count the passing time, would damage the hope they held—this very hope made it impossible for them to make any firm resolve to go on alone. Maybe Vaca and Lope would come next spring. Spring followed spring. Five years passed; they remained with the Yguazes.

ESTEBAN CAME RUNNING to where Dorantes was gathering pecans. "Andrés, Andrés, a Spaniard is coming. The Indians have seen him." He was excited. "Come quickly. In this direction." They walked forward.

Coming around a great boulder they saw a man advancing rapidly. Alone. As he came nearer they recognized Vaca. At the sight, Dorantes's body started trembling violently. He sank to his knees. In the vastness of the wilderness, after five years, God's mercy had reunited them. It was a miracle.

Dorantes's trembling told Vaca that he had been given up for dead. Esteban brought Castillo. The three were now four.

"Lope and the others?"

"I shall tell you all."

The Spaniards sat and looked at one another. Vaca's presence made each one aware of the changes time had wrought. Their emaciated bodies bore the marks of diverse abuse. Their matted hair and unkempt beards gave them a savage, dangerous look; exposure to sun and wind had blotched their fair skins and covered their shoulders with reddish, scaly sores. Unaccustomed to nakedness, they had cast their skins twice a year like serpents. By contrast, Esteban was the least changed. His dark skin had not been vulnerable to the elements, nor did his still-short hair look wild. Vaca kept looking at Esteban as though he was seeing him for the first time.

"I want to stay here with you. Will they accept another slave?" Vaca asked, well aware that another person might overtax their short food supplies.

"We shall see," Dorantes answered. "For the present it is their season of plenty. They are happy eating and busy with their festivals."

The Indians danced and sang through the night as Vaca told his story. "I will try to tell everything as it happened, but it is hard to remember with precision when I had neither paper nor inkpot and my main concern was to get the next meal. You know—some events are clear, some vague. So it is.

"Lope and I returned to the island with the Capoques. They no longer asked us to heal. It must have been one of you whom they considered the medicine-man—that is the only way I can account for their changed manner. They forced us to dig roots for the group who sat mourning, unable to feed themselves. The constant digging of roots from their bed beneath the salt water caused my fingers to bleed at the slightest touch. Such work and the harsh treatment I received made me long for death, the fate of our few comrades. I decided I had nothing to lose by flight. But I postponed it month after month in the hope

Lope would come with me. Thus it was a whole year before I made my way to the Charruco who inhabit the forests and much of the mainland coast.

"I think it was my misery that helped me find the way to live. You see, to escape is easy however dangerous it may be; but unless one finds a way to live, one just exchanges one misery for another. I kept thinking, how can I turn my weakness to strength. My weakness was being alone, being a stranger in any group I joined. My fair skin, my blond hair and long reddish beard made my strangeness instantly noticeable. While digging up the hated roots my mind was seeking a way to change this weakness to strength. Do you follow my thoughts?"

The three nodded, impatient for Vaca to get on with the story.

"You know, Esteban, it was when I remembered that you told how you had become a trader after fleeing from Azamor that I found the answer I had been seeking. I became a trader. In this region where each group is armed against every other group, except for brief truce periods, here where warfare is unrelenting, the traffic of goods becomes impossible. Such is the very heavy price these people pay to maintain their hostilities.

"When I came to the Charruco, I announced that I would seek merchandise outside their territory. Instantly they begged me to secure much-needed articles for which they yearned. So eager were they, they themselves furnished the goods I was to take inland. From the seashore I carried cones and other pieces of the shells of sea snails, conches from which they fashion knives, and a beanlike fruit especially prized for its curing properties. I bartered these with the interior tribes and in exchange secured items desired by the coastal tribes—skins, the reddish ochre they smear on their faces, hard canes suitable for arrows, flints for arrowheads, the sinew and cement to attach them, and deerhair, which they dye red and make into tassels.

"Being a trader suited me well. I went into the interior as far as I pleased, and perhaps a hundred miles along the coast. I had no master. The Indians were always glad to see me and were pleased when I arrived and brought them things they desired. They fed me. I became well known; other tribes who heard of me sent women to invite me to visit them.

"I need not tell you of the perils and privations, of the fear and the endless loneliness. Often storms and intense cold came upon me when I was by myself in the wilderness—but I survived by the great mercy of Our Lord. Also I soon adopted the ways of the Indians who in the winter retire to their buhíos, and lying under deerskins close to the fire, hibernate, torpid and incapable of exertion.

"In all those years of trading I ranged along the coast and went far inland, I sought to learn of two things: the path to Pánuco and news of the men in the other boats. When I heard about you three, I knew that with Lope only five men of our boats were still alive. What of the others? By questioning the many tribes I encountered I hoped to hear of survivors living among them. Many Indians had some bit to tell—either what they knew at first hand or what they had heard. Again and again I was amazed at how, in this land where there are no roads, no writing, tribes far away have intelligence of events. Often I found that tribes I knew nothing about were awaiting my arrival. But to get on with the grim facts.

"I have lived too long alone with pitiful ghosts. Strange, that I who saw the tens of thousands killed at Ravenna, where the battlefield was carpeted with the dead and dying, should be unable to free myself of thoughts of our comrades. Soldiers know there is a strong likelihood they will get killed—but the men of the expedition had great hopes. Ah, well," and Vaca sighed at the thought of what he had to tell.

"What happened to the men of the other three boats?" Vaca paused for a moment before beginning. "Narváez's rowers won their struggle to reach land. Taking no chances of being swept out to sea again, the boat hugged the shore and so came to a deep bay. There he was astonished to meet up with Friar Juarez, the notary, and those men of Boat Two who had managed to escape drowning when their boat had capsized in a wild, treacherous cross-current. You will want to know how many men escaped. At one time I too thought it important." Vaca looked away from his friends; he continued. "In the final tally, it really does not matter how many men saved themselves from death then. The survivors were like you—when their boat sank they lost everything but the clothes on their backs. Taking in his boat as many as he could, Narváez ferried them to the opposite shore and returned for the rest. Because day was ending and his own men were utterly exhausted, Narváez decided to resume the ferrying in the morning.

"That night his crew shared their pitiful little with the others. Then all stretched out on the beach. Except Narváez. He chose to sleep in the boat, keeping the coxswain with him and his little page who was too sick to move. Some time during the night while the men, spent and oblivious, slept, the boat quietly floated away. Out to sea. It had neither food nor water. When the men awoke they saw no boat—only the mark where the too-light stone anchor had been pulled—and though they looked and looked the sea was empty. The boat with its cargo had disappeared beyond the horizon. In my mind I see Narváez's dreadful awakening. In such manner the career and life of Don Pánfilo ended." His words sounded as though he were reading an epitaph cut in stone.

Vaca was silent. The night was filled with the sound of the Indians' songs as they feasted and visited and enjoyed their happy season.

"The men, undaunted, kept walking until the bay narrowed. They crossed it on a raft made God knows how out of driftwood. Rejoining the others, they finally came to a point of woods. A group of Mariames who had been camping there saw them coming and quickly loaded their canoes with all their goods and paddled away. Our comrades took over the Indian campsite—it had water and fuel at hand, and nearby they found crabs and shellfish. Winter had come with its cold; they decided to stay there.

"I shall tell you how our comrades, filled with hope and

capable of courage, died. Their number diminished steadily one by one of cold and hunger. The living dried and ate the flesh of those who died. God will forgive the terrible need that permitted them to do this. How He judged them, I do not know; the Mariames were horrified. In this way one man managed to live into March when an Indian returned to see how the party had made out. He took the sole survivor with him. Years had passed when the Indian told me this. I asked where the Spaniard was. When he had tried to escape, his master said, he tracked him down and killed him. This completed the score: not a single man from Boats One and Two is alive.

"The men in Boat Four were saved a lingering ordeal." There was almost a note of relief in Vaca's voice. "The storm that scattered us carried them toward the territory of the Camones. But first they drifted and drifted—water gone, food gone, and the cold robbing them of their strength. All of them, even the Captains Peñalosa and Tellez who had been so robust and active, were dying when their boat was finally washed ashore. Thus the Camones found them. What could they give them? It was their season of greatest scarcity. They did the merciful thing—they killed the men swiftly." And then Vaca added as though the words still broke his heart, "The Indians were sorrowful when they told me that not a single man had the strength to cry out."

The four sat without speaking, mourning their dead comrades. And again their ears heard only the Indians' song.

"And Lope? Is he dead too?" Castillo asked.

"I will tell you about Lope. I myself know what happened to him. Because he hesitated to leave the Capoques, I stayed in that locality for five years. Every year I would return to the island; every year I begged him to come with me so that we could start our quest for Christians. He put me off each year, promising we should start in the coming year. His excuse was that he could not swim. This became my concern. It was not simple, but finally I got him across to the mainland. We met some Indians—they call themselves the Deaguanes—and with them we went westward. You too crossed the four rivers that cut the coastline and know the bay we came to, wide and everywhere very deep. While the warriors of the Deaguanes stayed on the near side, we crossed with the women. They are good paddlers. On the other side were the Quevanes, who were coming to trade with our group.

"It was from the Quevanes that we heard about you. They spoke of you; described each of you; I could even catch your names. They even told us how badly you had been treated by the Mariames. I asked about the country ahead. They described it as poor country that provided nothing to eat, there were few people and that these, having no deerskins, suffered intensely from the cold. I was wondering in which direction to go, when they mentioned that when the pecans were ripe, your masters would be bringing you to the grove. They told me where that was.

"I cannot understand what changed them. For whatever reason they suddenly began to abuse us—they punched and kicked us, beat us with sticks and pelted us with stones and clumps of mud. When our jumping around no longer amused them, they would point an arrow against our chests and threaten to shoot. Then they laughed as we stood still and tense, the colour draining from our faces, while the archer was deciding whether or not to let the arrow fly.

"This deadly game proved too much for Lope. My comrade, who had been the strongest and the most stout-hearted man in my boat, could not endure this. He became fearful and piteous. Even sleep gave him no relief—he cried out as nightmares tormented him. He longed to return to the island. I pleaded with him, exhorted him. No, no, no, no—was his only answer. When, after a time, the women we had come with returned to the other shore, he followed them. I watched him dutifully shoulder a heavy load and sit in the canoe. That was the last I saw of him. He never even turned to look at me.

"Poor Lope! What had become of his courage? After he left and I was alone with the Quevanes, and all the time I was coming here, I wondered if I would find you or have to go on alone. Thoughts of Lope filled my mind and heart. What happened to his courage?"

"Bravery on the battlefield is not enough. It is easier to fight the Indians than to hold to a purpose like ours while trying to live with them," Dorantes said. "How could a man choose to remain a slave?"

That was all. No one else spoke. It was late; the excitement of the reunion left them spent.

T HE BEGINNING was hardly auspicious. Dorantes's master would not accept Vaca as a slave, nor would any other of the Yguazes. Already the nights were cold; winter would soon come.

"I shall return to the Quevanes. I do not think they will kill me," Vaca said. "If they let me stay with them, I shall be abused and endure hunger, but there will be a spot in a fire-warmed buhío where I can sleep. Since our masters come together for the prickly pear season, we shall be able to escape together."

"We have taken an oath to reach Pánuco," Dorantes said. "With you the quest becomes possible."

"Don Álvar Núñez," Esteban added, "help us plan how we are to effect our passage through all the Indian groups. As a trader you found your path open and the Indians friendly. But on a one-way passage we cannot act as traders. Not only are we naked and unarmed, we are without wares. If there is something they want and need, our quest would be easier."

"Esteban is right. But what merchandise could we carry?" Dorantes asked.

"I cannot think of anything that would always be welcome," Vaca answered. "But Esteban has a valuable idea. We must try to find goods that everyone wants."

"It will be another six months before the prickly pear season begins. In that time we should be able to find an answer," Castillo said. "One word of caution, Don Álvar Núñez: let me counsel you as I counsel myself. There are three rules to observe—first, patience; second, patience;

third, patience. When we meet again there must not be even a whisper that we mean to escape."

"Never ask the Yguazes what lies beyond their territory," Dorantes said, "nor what people there are, nor what the nature of the land is. They must feel we are content being reunited. Then they will relax their vigilance."

Esteban added his word of caution, "Let it appear that your only aim is to please your master. Confine your dissatisfactions to your hunger. They understand the misery of an empty stomach."

"I shall be on my guard," Vaca promised.

"Then it is agreed. We shall meet again at the place of the prickly pear. It covers a large area, and people from farther west come there to barter and eat. When we have escaped from the part frequented by the Yguazes, we can accompany the other groups." This was the plan Dorantes had designed. It met with the approval of the others.

They separated; they had but six months to wait to begin their quest.

Patience, patience, patience—endlessly the leaden months, cold, bleak, and filled with unsatisfied hunger, dragged out their full span of days. And then, it was the time of the prickly pear.

As the different groups converged on the fields filled with bright, luscious food, the Quevanes and Yguazes met at the very approach to the site. Almost at the very place and time Dorantes had planned that their escape would begin. Just there, just then, a sudden quarrel over a woman started the two groups fighting. Screaming curses and insults, they fought—a free-for-all, fists, sticks, hitting, beating, punching, whacking, poking, thrusting, kicking—until bruised and bloody they drew apart. Each group went back over the path it had come. The four had only a brief moment together: *Next Year!*

Patience, patience, patience. Taken utterly by surprise, they had to wait another year before they could meet again. They were convinced that the only way they could make their way westward was in the company of returning Indians.

Again the happy season had come, bringing together Indians from many parts. This time nothing marred the meeting; the four arranged how and when they would escape. That same night another quarrel broke out and the Indians determined to separate in the morning. Vaca found his friends in a patch of prickly pear snatching some fruit before they left.

"I shall not wait another year," he said, and there was finality in his voice. "I waited for Lope in vain; I shall not wait on the Indians' good humour. Tonight we will have the new moon. In seven days, before the crescent becomes full, I shall return to this same spot. I shall wait here a week after the full moon. No longer. If by that time you do not come, I shall go on alone."

The moon was to be their calendar. It was the eighth of September and the year was 1534. A full six years had passed since they left the Bay of Horses.

They parted; the place and time was set for their re-union and escape.

Vaca was the first to reach the appointed place. Some Indians were still there gathering the last of the prickly pears. During the day he hid and ventured out when it was dark to collect some fruit that served as both food and drink. It was safe then, for with twilight the air grew cold and the Indians sat cozily in their fire-warmed buhíos. In his isolated spot, Vaca kept his naked body warm by lighting two fires and sitting between them. The chill night air served as his watchman, waking him when his fires needed replenishing.

On the thirteenth day Dorantes and Esteban came.

"We had the most absurd obstacles and misadventures. Thank God you are still here," Dorantes blurted out, shaking his head at the thought that they might have arrived too late.

"We got lost," Esteban added, as though it was something to be ashamed of. "We were lucky to meet some Indians. I think they call themselves Lanegados. To make sure we would not miss you Alonso stayed with them. We ran ahead once they set us on the right path. They will be here tomorrow."

"Let us celebrate," Vaca said happily. "We have the time, we have the drink." They squeezed the ripe fruit, letting the juice run into a hole dug in the ground. When their punch bowl was full they took turns drinking, toasting their reunion, their freedom, and the hope they held.

"No wine ever tasted better," Dorantes said when they had drunk their fill and lay on a rock, warmed by the sun. After a long pause he continued. "Don Álvar Núñez, this past year I have thought much about my plan for escape. We all thought it was fine, that nothing could go wrong. Not one of us could have foreseen that it would be wrecked by a senseless quarrel which robbed the Indians of their cherished prickly pear plenty. That quarrel was against everything I had counted on."

"What can we learn from this?" Vaca asked.

"It has taught me that plans are useful only if they can be changed as the situation changes," Dorantes answered.

"Andrés," Esteban said, "in my country we had a proverb for just such events. 'Tomorrow may not be the future you planned today.'"

"Let us not plan. God will show us our way," Vaca said.

Two days later Castillo joined them. They were together: the four. They were jubilant at their success, excited at the prospect of starting on their long-delayed quest. They were alive, ready to face the unknown. They knew how far they had come since they were helpless castaways. They also knew that the next day could bring them death. The Yguazes and Quevanes would not let them live if they were caught. They slept uneasily.

Their escape began like a rout. As soon as the first glimmer of light showed them the east, they commended themselves to God and began their flight. Where? To the west—that was the one fact they knew. To whom? They did not know. There was an initial urgency for speed, speed, and ever greater speed: better let their lungs burst than be overtaken. They gained strength and mounting hope as hour after hour the sun moved majestically across the sky and they kept putting miles of safety between them and the slavery they had endured. Somewhere, they knew, they had passed out of the territory of their masters; soon they could expect to meet new groups.

Late in the afternoon they saw thin fingers of smoke rising straight in the still air, as though signals sent up for their guidance. They headed for them, careful to make no sound. Suddenly, without warning, they met an Indian. He started running as they advanced toward him. They stopped. He stopped. They looked at one another.

"Stay here," Esteban said. "Let me go alone and speak with him."

Seeing one man advancing alone, the Indian stopped; Esteban talked. "We are seeking the men whose fires we see." He repeated it again and again while the Indian looked at the four strangers. They carried no weapons; they could not be a war party. But there were no women with them, so they could not be intent on trade or festivities. "We have come a long way in search of you. We come in peace; we come in peace."

Beckoning them to follow, the Indian went ahead to

announce their approach. Twilight was almost ended and the cold was strong when they reached the encampment. Four Indians stood on the path.

"We bid you welcome," one of them said. Their language was similar to that of the Mariames, but they shared none of their malevolence.

"We have come a long distance to be with you," Vaca said, matching the Indians' gracious welcome by assuming the dignity of a guest. Their words and manner pleased their hosts. They escorted the four inside the encampment. Vaca and Castillo were led to the buhío of one medicine man, Dorantes and Esteban to that of another. To be lodged with a medicine man was a great honour; it also indicated what the Indians considered them to be. Discreet questions and cautious answers on both sides gradually disclosed the situation into which the four wanderers had miraculously come.

"We have come to the very people we hoped to meet at the place of the prickly pear." Esteban was relating what he had learned to the others. "They are the group to the west of the Yguazes, those from whom they obtain their bows and arrows. But Don Álvar Núñez, we are fortunate that these two groups have been kept apart by quarrels for two seasons."

"Something is puzzling you—what?" Vaca asked.

"They never saw us as slaves. They think that we are supernatural beings who came out of nowhere to find them. How can that be? To be healers, yes; but gods?"

"The Lord God is merciful," Vaca answered. "It *is* possible, Esteban. I remember hearing what happened to

Cortés when he arrived at Mexico. The Aztec emperor did not know whether Cortés was the great god whose return the seers had foretold. It seems that Cortés stepped ashore on the very day appointed for the god. Even so mighty and learned a priest-emperor could not determine whether Cortés was the god come to re-establish his divine rule or an enemy come to conquer his empire.

"As I see it, though our arrival seems very different to us—we seek passage not dominion, we are naked and unarmed, we are but four—to them the choice is between gods and slaves. How else can they explain our presence? It is God's will that they regard us as gods."

Castillo, deeply perplexed, asked, "Must we chose between being a god or a slave? Is it not possible to be a man?"

WITH THESE INDIANS, who called themselves the Avavares, the mysterious and moving part of their quest began. Slowly, almost unwillingly, they were about to discover the commodity valued everywhere.

The very next day a few Avavares addressed themselves to Castillo. They complained of severe pains in their heads and begged him to cure them. He could not deny their entreaties; he knelt and said an Our Father and then stood up and made the sign of the cross over them. Instantly they announced that all pain was gone. The camp bubbled with a lively joy, laughter was heard;

and the cured men ran to their buhíos to return bearing a supply of prickly pears. One brought a small piece of venison, a delicacy the four ex-slaves had not tasted until then.

News of Castillo's healing spread. That night many more came beseeching him to cure them, each bringing a piece of venison. When the ceremony was finished, the four crowded into Vaca's buhío to thank God for His compassion and mercy and goodness to them, while outside, all night, the Avavares danced and sang in praise of the gods who had come to them.

When after three days and nights the festivities ended, the four questioned their hosts about the country to the west, its tribes, and on what they lived. The information had a discouraging familiarity: the prickly pear abounded, and when its season was over, almost all the people returned to scattered territories. Great cold lay over that region, and unlike the Avavares, those who dwelt there had few skins with which to keep warm. Faced with such dismal prospects, and with winter about to grip the land, the four decided to stay where they were.

Counting the moons, they were with the Avavares for eight months, of which six were passed in dire want.

Avavares from all parts came seeking help for ills that afflicted them. Unerringly—so specific were the details given—they came to Castillo. But even as his fame and success grew, so did his misgivings. He became reluctant to attempt cases which he deemed very serious, and made the others join him in the curing ceremony. Deeper and deeper grew his belief that he was sinning and that God would punish him for his sins. The crisis came when some Susoles, a nearby tribe, sent for him to come. They urged haste, for among their sick was one who seemed very near his end.

Castillo flatly refused to go. He still refused though his friends urged him to accept the call since so much rested on their ability to cure.

"Alonso," Vaca addressed him without pleading or reproach, "if you fear for your soul, if your sins weigh upon you, I cannot argue against your refusal. I, however, though equally culpable as a sinner, am of a different opinion. We must answer this call. We *must* because I believe that we are the humble instruments of Providence. Until God shows me that I am *not* His creature performing His will, I will keep trying to heal. It is not for me to try and fathom God's will: If I offend Him, He will declare it with terrible certainty.

"I will answer this call. Andrés, Esteban, will you come with me?" The three started for the Susoles' camp. They walked quickly, for it was at a distance and the call had been urgent. Some Avavares went with them to show the way.

As they approached the camp, all evidence indicated that the patient had died. As was customary among the Indians, his buhío had been pulled down, and surrounded by his weeping family, he lay under a mat. Vaca pulled the mat down and saw the eyes rolled up; he could feel no pulse. "He is dead," Vaca thought, so too did Dorantes and Esteban. Notwithstanding, they pulled the mat completely off, laid their hands on him, and prayed. Fervently they prayed, and long, they breathed on him many times and blessed him. When they were through with the ceremony, the family presented Vaca with the bow of the dead man and also a basket of pounded prickly pear.

Many others in the camp also lay ill, in a kind of stupor. The three visited each one, to pray and bless. For this ceremony, two more baskets of pounded prickly pear were offered to Vaca. These he turned over to the Avavares who had guided them and who, when the three returned to the Avavares tribe, remained behind with the Susoles. When, later, these also returned, they brought startling news: the man mourned as dead, the one they had considered lifeless, had stood up well and whole, had eaten and chatted. A quiver of excitement passed from buhío to buhío as the witnesses of this miraculous healing related the events again and again. Wonder and fear spread abroad through the land.

People spoke of nothing else. Daily, new groups came to experience the health the four brought and asked to have their children blessed; those who arrived sick became well. A contagion of well-being swept through the camp. Relief and reassurance, reinforced with each cure, led inevitably to the conviction that no one would die while the miracle workers stayed in their midst. Thus it happened that the four castaways found their new role. They had become the Healers who banished sickness.

"We must make plans," Vaca said to his companions. "Summer is near. In a month or two the prickly pear will begin to ripen. I think our stay here has been long enough —we must start for Pánuco."

"Will they permit us to leave?" Dorantes asked. "Sometimes I feel as though the great confidence we inspire has become a kind of prison."

"They say the tribe farthest west of whom they know anything is the Maliacones," Vaca said, his mind still busy with planning. "Also they say that except for the season of the prickly pear, they hunger most of the year."

"Hunger is hunger," Castillo said. "We are experts in that subject. I know that if the Maliacones can endure it, so can we." And then, suddenly, he spoke from his heart. "Don Álvar Núñez, I am ashamed that I ever doubted God's goodness. Like the Avavares and Susoles I have had proof of His presence and enduring mercy. I no longer feel I am lost in a wilderness. Rather, as my professor of theology was in the habit of saying, I am in the 'sack of Providence.' If God wills, we shall be delivered from it safely."

"Well spoken, Alonso. God has shown us that as physicians we are welcome and respected. And of immense use to these half-starved, frightened people. We have also discovered the way four men, naked and unarmed, can traverse this vast New World."

"Don Álvar Núñez, Andrés, Alonso," Esteban suddenly said. "Listening to you has given me an idea. You keep saying that as physicians we are welcome and respected. But the Indians whom we have healed and blessed do not think of us as physicians, to them we are supernaturals to whom they make offerings of food and whatever else precious they possess. When we first met the Avavares you, Don Álvar Núñez, did not relate our trials and escape—you merely said that we had come a great distance to find them. Our coming was unexpected, as is proper for gods, and so should our going be."

"How easy to see things only one way. Of course, you are right, Esteban. We must stop seeing ourselves through our own eyes. The Indians hold up their mirror —we must learn to look into it."

The next morning, without the Indians being aware of it, Vaca and Esteban walked until they found the Maliacones. Three days later Esteban returned and guided Dorantes and Castillo to where Vaca awaited them.

They had moved beyond the groups of Indians Vaca had heard of during his years of trading in the interior. They had, they realized, crossed a kind of boundary between what they knew and what was unknown. It was the first giant step in their quest for Christians.

As the Avavares had said, the region was a poor one with half-famished groups. From the Maliacones, who got some nourishment from the fruit of the red barberry while waiting for the prickly pear to ripen, they passed to the Arbadaos. These showed the tragic effects of prolonged, extreme want—their limbs were shrunken and their bellies bloated. With them the four suffered more intensely than with any other group.

They had indeed learned how to survive. To permit the Indians who knew the meagre resources of their territory to give all their time to food gathering, the four earned their way by weaving mats for the buhíos, by fashioning bows and arrows and nets, and by scraping the skins of whatever game was procured. By such tasks they earned food—a poor, poor diet. Occasionally they were given tidbits of meat, which they chewed raw, and they feasted on what fat and tissue they scraped off the skins.

They did not starve, but they began to lose strength. So that they would not sink into a lethargy, Vaca bartered the large skin he covered himself with at night for two dogs. These provided a satisfying, substantial meal.

Restored, they pushed on. How will we be received? What role will we be expected to play? Questions filled their minds as they walked forward.

4 / The Procession

VACA AND HIS COMPANIONS had wandered off the path pointed out to them by the Indians. It had rained all day. When night fell, they made a good bonfire and camped. They moved occasionally, turning to warm themselves.

"I am beginning to enjoy this New World," said Esteban with his back to the fire. "I feel good: the rain washed me and this fire warms me. And it's good to know that in the morning we will have the prickly pear leaves now roasting. I feel like a boy again. Why, the wilderness even feels like a home."

"I too, Esteban," Dorantes chimed in. "I think it's because I really believe we are on our way home. At last we are going where we want. I never felt as lost as when we were castaways."

"For me," Castillo said, "just not being a slave—that is wonderful." And he added as an afterthought, "Poor Lope! I still cannot imagine that he was willing to be a slave just for the right to live. Terrible. With God's help we shall go on as physicians. However, I prefer to consider myself a trader selling health, the item everyone needs and wants. See, Don Álvar, how much I have learned in this university?"

"Castaways, slaves, physicians, or traders if you want that word—how we have worked our way up," Vaca remarked. "I feel at home, but I do not feel like a native."

"When you list the roles we have played, you make us sound like strolling players," Esteban laughed. "How do you think the next group will cast us?"

"We shall soon find out."

No longer in flight, no longer unable to fend for themselves, the four were on the eve of assuming their heroic role. The walk was about to become a procession. Unannounced and unaccompanied, they came at evening to a large encampment. "Peace, peace," Vaca repeated. Their unexpected appearance and looks threw the inhabitants into a nervous commotion.

Were they apparitions? Slowly, guardedly, the Indians looked at their visitors. Timidly they came closer, close enough to reach out and pass their hands first over the strangers' faces and bodies, and then, in like manner, over their own. Flesh and form, muscle, bone, movement—they established their bodily existence and human likeness.

News of their curing powers must have spread ahead of them, for the next morning the Indians brought them their sick, beseeching them to heal and bless. Gladly they offered their entire supply of roasted leaves and green fruit. Among the others who quickly came to see the miracle workers was a group who indicated they had travelled a great distance from the west to benefit from the physicians' services. Because that was the direction they wanted to take, Vaca and his companions decided to accompany them when they returned home.

In the encampment of their new hosts, after the children had been assembled and blessed, they were offered not the customary prickly pears but a new staple—quantities of mesquite-bean flour.

"It has a wholesome taste," Dorantes pronounced after trying some. "A little coarse and gritty, but sweet. Almost like the almond paste of Andalusia. What is it? Does anyone know?"

"From a fruit. It looks like Saint John's bread; it also puckers the mouth. I tasted it uncooked. How do they sweeten it?" Castillo asked.

"With earth," Vaca said. They looked to see if he was joking. "Isn't that so, Esteban? We watched them preparing it. They were pounding the long pods, husks, and seeds together. They keep adding earth as we would sugar. When the taste suits them, they simply add water —and have the paste you enjoy."

Handful by handful, the four ate, helping themselves from the pot. "How delicious the sugary taste is! It is a real celebration after all the prickly pears we have lived on," Castillo said, savouring each mouthful.

"I think for the Indians too it is a special treat. They are celebrating our presence," Esteban explained. "They are jubilant that in the morning we shall heal and bless." The four watched their hosts gathered in small groups around a pot, happily engrossed in stuffing themselves, gorging until their bellies swelled with the earth and water consumed.

"We have lived under the shadow of hunger long enough to know that there is no better way to express jubilation than by feasting." Vaca was serious as he ate the mesquite flour. "I have learned what a blessing it is to have the appetite satisfied once in a while."

"Very different from gluttony, the sin of the too-well fed," Castillo added. "But why the jubilation? Why the celebration? Nobody has made a festival like this before to welcome us?"

"I think I can answer that, Alonso," Esteban said. "As Don Álvar and I were walking around and looking, I also listened. They are talking about the presence of guardian spirits. They spoke of us with the same respect they have for spirits called Vulture and Talking Tree, Grey Spider Woman, and White Measuring Worm."

"Esteban, you are making this all up," Vaca said with mock seriousness. "Or, you are telling me that their gods are as miserable and misbegotten as their lives. In any case we are not vicious like the demon the Arbadaos called Bad Thing."

"That one they whispered about?" Castillo asked. "The one they were afraid to mention out loud? I remember him: he would appear like a bolt of lightening, slash his victim open, suck out his entrails and heart, and leave his victim to die. I remember we laughed him out of their fears."

"It was when we were able to destroy a demon just by laughing at him that I knew it was God's will for us to walk through the wilderness and bring peace and ease to these frightened people," Vaca said.

"So we are now guardian spirits," said Castillo, weighing the enormity of their masquerade. "Then, like Don Álvar, I say let us not betray Our Lord. Let us try hard to bring comfort and reassurance to men living in a world haunted by malign forces."

"Amen," said Dorantes and Esteban.

"Amen," said Vaca. And then he continued speaking, slowly and with emphasis. "That being so, I think it behoves us to act in a manner becoming this belief. I feel that their faith puts a heavy burden on us. We must not betray it."

"Do you mean we should refuse to heal and bless?"

"Quite the contrary, Andrés. I mean that when we were physicians we acted in the manner of their physicians even as we prayed to Our Lord and He showed us His compassion. Now they consider us to be guardian spirits. We cannot abuse their faith. We cannot deny it —that would serve no purpose and only confuse them. We must act as they expect such supernatural beings to act. The Indians practise continence before seeking divine help, therefore we must be continent; they fast before engaging in any activity which seeks divine help, therefore we must be abstemious."

Deeply moved, Castillo said, "Let us model ourselves on our own sweet Saint Francis: let us seek nothing for ourselves and keep our hearts and spirits open to God. He will point out our path to us and we shall be the humble instruments of His will."

Thus, in some measure, they were prepared to accept the role desired of them by the Indians.

THE PROCESSION'S BEGINNING did not give any hint of its rich flowering. An escort of women from the group they were leaving was joined by women who came from the next group to guide them directly to their large encampment. The trail was long; the sun was setting as they approached their new hosts. At the very sight of the four, the Indians began an ear-piercing ululation, a wild, ecstatic chorus, all the while striking their hands sharply against their thighs. Long, shrill cries above a rhythmic slapping: great anxiety and intense joy. Then came a rush of frenzied men and women, pushing and pressing and lunging forward to touch their celestial visitors. In such manner the mantle of divinity was fearfully thrown over the four.

For a moment it looked as though they would be knocked down and trampled. Suddenly—no one was quite sure how or by whom—each of the four was lifted up, and without being permitted to set foot on the ground, was carried into the encampment. Shocked by such a reception, they remained inside the buhíos that had been prepared for them, grateful for the privacy that allowed them to compose themselves for the coming day. Outside, the Indians sang their sacred songs and danced to honour gods who came bringing the longed-for promise of health and well-being. When the celebration ended at dawn, the four emerged to bestow their blessings and touch each man, woman, and child.

After the last Indian had passed before them, a man, well-built and with an assured manner, stepped forward. He held a gourd in his outstretched hands. He spoke to them. "Sacred Ones. This is a holy rattle. It comes from heaven. Occasionally, when the river is angry and rushes out from its banks, it leaves behind this precious gift. Much virtue resides in it. Much, much power. Only he who possesses strong medicine gained in a vision dare touch it. It speaks to us with the very voice of heaven. We honour it with our most sacred dances." He shook the rattle, and the people, hearing the sacred sound, trembled.

When he had finished, Vaca advanced slowly and solemnly to accept the gift. He examined the gourd, in which pebbles had been inserted through a hole, and held it aloft in his left hand as he made the sign of the cross. Then he shook it; the rattle spoke for him. At the conclusion of this formal presentation, the grateful inhabitants gave arrows to the women who had accompanied the four and were now eager to return to their tribe. The ceremony of gift giving to honour the passage of the celestial visitors was beginning to take form and assume importance. Vaca and his companions watched it, vaguely aware that an etiquette was evolving.

"Naked and poor as they are, they clothe their gods richly in acts that have meaning for them," Vaca said that night after they had eaten the one meal they had each day. "I marvel at the way they can create behaviour proper for an unusual event."

"If we respect their feeling for ceremony," Esteban said, "shouldn't we try to match it, Don Álvar?"

"You are right. Let me think a moment." And Vaca, remembering court behaviour as he had been taught it when a page in the ducal castle, said to the others, "Andrés and Alonso, you will receive whatever gifts the Indians make; you, Esteban, will be our spokesman, transmitting exchanges between the Indians and their gods. I shall be the unapproachable, inaccessible one, neither dealing with nor speaking to them except through others. It is advantageous to keep a reserve of sacred power. It adds distance and mystery and may prove useful. As a soldier I witnessed senseless, useless campaigns in which many died and nothing was achieved. I'll wager that the silence of a dissatisfied god will prove louder than cannon and his immobility more powerful than a cavalry charge."

Having assigned the parts each would play, they felt easier about meeting new ceremonies.

When they left the next day, the entire body of Indians accompanied them. As before, they were received by the next tribe with wild rejoicing and were offered their choicest food—fresh deer shot that day. Here an additional ceremony was incorporated into the procession: the Indians who followed them took the bow and arrows, the sandals, the beads, if he wore any, from each one of the new group who desired to be cured and blessed. When they had stripped him of his possessions they led him to the four to be healed. The patient was undisturbed at being robbed; rather he seemed content, and soon happily proclaimed that he was well.

As they advanced, again and again this ceremony of tearful farewells and joyous welcome, of blessing and curing, of patients made well and whole, of night-long singing and dancing continued. The ceremonies had become established; both Indians and divine guests followed the roles they had designed and perfected.

Only the cold-blooded pilfering of property was a disturbing custom which the four could not understand.

"What an outlandish march this is," Castillo remarked when they were resting in a new encampment. "Is it a pilgrimage? No, since it is the object of worship that moves. I think ours is a religious procession making its way through many different groups—different languages and customs."

"Those differences are unimportant," Dorantes said. "The Indians are united in their common hope for good health; they all desire to be freed from the fears that assail them. Word of our presence has spread, and with it the ceremonies that are proper to our coming and going."

"It is incredible, Alonso," Esteban said, "that the procession continues without faltering through all these different groups even though the marchers change with the scenery. I never saw or heard of a procession like ours. Have you, Don Álvar?"

Vaca shook his head in wonderment. "I, too, am amazed. Though the marchers change from day to day, the customs never do. Men and women carry on and perform ceremonies that were designed the day before, or whose beginnings took place far, far from their homes. I'll wager that we have not seen the end of their capacity to create ceremonies."

Vaca was right. Quite soon after this another innovation was added. The four were badly alarmed the first time it happened.

As usual, they arrived at the new group's encampment

escorted by those with whom they had stayed the previous night; as usual there was the excited, joyous welcome. Without losing time or asking permission, their former hosts began stripping the inhabitants of whatever they wore or carried, and unsatisfied, swarmed through the buhíos leaving them empty—bare. Aghast, the four helplessly watched the systematic looting of hosts who had received them so hospitably. They, noticing the distress and dismay of the celestial visitors, sought to reassure them. One of them, his arms filled with goods, addressed them. "Sacred Ones, do not grieve for them." And then the man who had spoken the words of welcome when they arrived, added his words. "Let there be joy on your faces as there is in our hearts. The sight of you is all the riches we want or need. We are glad to give everything we have to those who guide you to us. Rejoice as we rejoice." And then he said, as though everything had been planned and arranged, "We shall regain more than we have lost when we escort you to those on ahead. They are very rich."

"I accept the explanation but cannot understand it," Esteban said in a puzzled way. "When I was a trader, it was the men who made handsome profits who lamented most when their purses were picked and they lost pennies. This is just the opposite."

By one act and then another, the ceremony built up, yet the new elaborations seemed known to those ahead as well as to those who had begun it. The newly plundered Indians escorted their guests to the next group who, although closely related, were raided as though they had been enemies. In turn, the new victims insisted on guiding their visitors toward another friendly group—they did not want enemies to profit from the blessings and ministrations brought to them.

At one encampment, the inhabitants offered the four their most precious possessions—beads beautifully wrought out of shell, ochre brought from a great distance, and several little bags filled with glittering mica. Castillo and Dorantes accepted the gifts and brought them to Vaca, who blessed them and handed them back so that they could be distributed among their escort. In this manner the four initiated their own ceremony of blessing and and distributing all offerings.

The country through which they passed began to change. A few days later the four caught their first glimpse of distant mountains.

"Ah, the mountains." Vaca looked at them in salutation. "Though far away, they are a promise of a successful end to our quest." And he explained that New Spain must lie in that direction since Cortés had scaled mountains when he marched from the coastal plain toward the great city, the rich, proud city of the Aztecs. At the same encampment, as if to verify their approaching proximity to New Spain, they had their first sight and taste of maize flour. It spoke to them of Mexico and reunion with Christians. In response to a question from Esteban, the Indians told them that the flour had come from far away and had cost them many bags of mica. "Where?" he asked again. They pointed inland, due west, in the direction of the river which flowed straight from the mountains.

Due west: toward the setting sun. This was their direction.

When, the next morning, the Indians insisted on escorting them in another direction where they would find settlements that were large and prosperous, they refused. "We must go there, where the sun sets," Esteban announced. The Indians warned that the region to the west was poor and supported few inhabitants. "We must go toward the setting sun," Esteban repeated. "There is our home."

Where the paths forked, they parted. Regretfully, reluctantly, the Indians turned down the river to their encampment while the four followed the river as it led upward. The procession had suddenly, unexpectedly ended. Determined to keep to the west and undaunted at being alone, the four pushed on. A poor country it was, as the Indians had described it. Once again they were dependent on prickly pears. It was the late summer and they were ripe for eating.

Alone, the four arrived at a very small encampment; there were only a score of buhíos. They were greeted with weeping and cries of lamentation. They were perplexed but not worried by this unusual behaviour, even though heretofore crying and weeping had marked their departure. But when the Indians saw that their guests were quite alone, with no pillaging escort, they dried their tears, stilled their cries, and grudgingly offered a few prickly pears.

Night came. It was quiet. There were no night-long celebrations with sacred songs and dances to disturb their sleep. What, the four wondered, did this new attitude forebode? They talked it over to no avail. Must they find a new way to pass through the unknown wilderness in their quest for Christians? How could the procession suddenly melt away? They had become accustomed to it, seeing it as a mysterious instrument of God's mercy: it had smoothed their path and brought peace and health and joy to those Indians who, for a short time, marched with them. The quiet of the night was more disturbing than the customary noise.

At dawn, the Indians from whom they had parted the day before, broke into the encampment. The unsuspecting inhabitants, supposing themselves safe from pillage, had concealed nothing. As they saw the determined looting, they wept long and very loud. One of the looters stopped and addressed them. "What are you that you cry? What manner of men are you that you do not recognize the Children of the Sun? You should rejoice that they are with you while they journey to their home yonder— there where the sun lives." Having silenced them, he continued. "Anger them not. Theirs is the power to heal; theirs, too, the power to destroy. Respect such supernatural power. Offend them in no way. Offer them gladly whatever you possess and their stay among you will bring great good. Guide the holy four to those who are many and have much and you will receive all they have. The sun, who daily climbs the backbone of the sky, has sent us his four sons, the sacred number, that we may recognize they are gods."

The Indians zealously followed the advice given them, heaping more on those already burdened with the goods they had pilfered. They attended the Children of the Sun with awe, reverence, and eager consideration and escorted them to the next large encampment—a long three-day march. Messengers sped ahead to announce and instruct so that the ceremonies proper to their passage would be observed.

Among the gifts offered at the new settlement were two sacred rattles venerated for their curing powers. These, together with the one they had first received, were used in all their curing ceremonies. They were also presented with a copper bell. Thick, large, with a haunting face moulded on one side, it was a treasured possession. Dorantes, who received it, asked Esteban to inquire whence it came. From neighbours, the Indians said; neighbours who received it from their neighbours leading all the way to the north. Much copper was found there, they added, and everywhere it was highly esteemed. They also reported that the people did not live in buhíos but in permanent habitations.

As though sounding faintly out of their long-buried dreams, the copper bell spoke to the Spaniards of kingdoms wherein were to be found mines and foundries and skilled metal-working artisans; of cities and wealth. How strong is the stuff of dreams. Not La Florida, nor enduring hunger, nor mean slavery could stop the golden hope of the New World.

"I confess," said Dorantes, holding the bell so that it would not ring and looking at the stark face that peered back at him from the bell, "I find this has a mysterious and moving quality. Can it be called art? The face says so much yet it lacks the beauty of our carving. Or is it simply the metal that calls up instantly the hopes I thought forever killed by our excursion in La Florida?"

"You speak of La Florida," Castillo said, holding the copper bell in turn, "and I almost hear a note of regret in your voice. As for me, I find being in a procession much easier than being in an expedition. Hearing the Indians' jubilant welcome is more to my liking than the whine of their deadly arrows. I pray I am not falling into sin when I admit that I would rather be a Child of the Sun than a captain in anyone's army."

"For the moment I am content to be a Child of the Sun instead of Treasurer and High-Sheriff of La Florida. But," Vaca admitted, "the moment will be over when I am back in Spain. What astonishes me is the fluency with which the Indians lie. Aren't we Children of the Sun because they are liars? Or am I too harsh? Should I say rather they possess rich imaginations? True, the procession works wonderfully well for us, but I keep feeling I am caught in a kind of galloping rigmarole. I suppose I never expected people so utterly destitute to be so rich in imagination. Yet how faulty my logic is: no one could have been poorer than the rich, well-favoured Don Pánfilo, God rest his soul."

"And I," said Esteban, holding the bell and talking to the intense face, "I think that being a god and being a slave have something in common. Neither is considered to be human, that is, to be a man like other men. True, one is above and the other below, but both are treated as nonhuman."

"Esteban," Castillo said in an excited voice, "I am sure you are right. The Indians have only those two categories to fit us into. We are like the gourds: they are alien to this region and come when the river is in flood—*ergo*, they are from heaven. Similarly, we who are, so to speak, washed up on their territory are either debris or divine. Very neat logic. Is that what you mean?"

"Yes, but you put it so .well, Alonso. I also feel that they are not saying we are Children of the Sun to deceive anyone. They are not liars. It is their way of fitting us into the uncommon, the unusual, the different-from-Indian. All their guardian spirits have names. Remember? Buzzard, West Wind, and even the demon they called Bad Thing. Names, names. Like handles. What is more natural for them to put two and two together. We bring good health and we insist on going to the west: Children of the Sun. It was so very different in Azamor—there spirits were nameless. Don Álvar, forgive me for wandering so. But to my ears their naming us Children of the Sun is a kind of poetry."

"What you have called poetry," Castillo said, "in the university we called myths. I remember our professor of rhetoric. Very eloquent and elegant in his discourse on the stories of the pagan gods and goddesses of ancient Rome. He called them myths which, he said, were explanations for what needs explaining, or, justifications for natural phenomena. He was pointing out how myths differ from our Gospels, God's Word revealed to man. He also said that myths have a life of their own."

"Between Azamor and the university, I have learned much. I thank both of you. I shall sleep now like a cherished, sacred rattle. This sun's son is going to set." And Dorantes, smiling, stretched out to sleep.

Vaca looked at him. "Our friend Andrés is amused and

relaxed. A good sign. I understood your correction, Esteban, and yours, too, Alonso. I accept that we are a myth. Fine. I accept that the myth justifies our procession and the procession is our safe-conduct pass for our quest through the wilderness. I pray that as Children of the Sun we may remain free from pride, vanity, and greed, and by serving Our Lord thank Him for His infinite compassion and mercy."

THE PROCESSION CONTINUED for weeks and months. Each day brought new meetings, sights, impressions, and adventures; but even novelty, endlessly repeated, loses its sharpness. The journey became a blur. The looting ceremony performed at each meeting was meticulously observed. Gradually they began to understand it. Seeing it through Indian eyes gave it a different meaning.

From conversations with the Indians, Esteban got the first clue. "Don Álvar," he explained, "we have been calling it looting, pilfering, sacking. Such words are the way we judged this behaviour. Their word means something very different, more like 'gift-giving' or 'giveaway.' It is as traditional and legitimate as the barter you and I both engaged in when we were traders."

"A glorified, grand-scale giveaway makes everyone content," Vaca replied. "It pleases those who give and those who receive. It must be pleasant to get rid of the old things and have everything brand-new."

Learning about the giveaway removed their last scruple; they knew that they were not leading looters, but men and women walking in the company of living gods who, by this ceremony, declared property only has uses but no value. A word, a gesture, a ceremony seen through the Indians' eyes was accepted by the four—the wilderness was changing their ideas and feelings.

No matter how humdrum the routines became, the four knew themselves to be living in a pristine world where gods and demigods strode the earth and talked and cared for suffering man. The procession was charged with a spiritual quality; in serving the Children of the Sun, the Indians made every commonplace act a way whereby blessings flowed out to each marcher. In turn, the four found themselves as deeply involved as the Indians in the myth of the Children of the Sun.

The profound change began in this fashion. During a routine welcome at a new encampment, a man was brought to be healed, a man whose sickness came from the exhausting pain of an arrow whose head had pierced his right shoulder and lodged itself close to his heart. He had suffered a long time; his every movement was an agony.

Vaca stepped forward to examine him. Gently, expertly, his fingers moved over the man's chest. "I must probe to see what can be done. I have often had to remove a bullet from one of my soldiers after a battle. Ah! I can just feel the arrowhead." He stood up. "It will be harder to get out than a bullet, but not impossible." With no fuss, Vaca prepared what he would need for the operation: his knife, a shell honed to a fine cutting edge; a deer-bone needle threaded with fine sinew; and some matted hair scraped from a deer hide. When everything was ready, he made an incision. He could see the embedded arrowhead—it was on an awkward slant. "I have to cut deeper." He touched it with the tip of his knife. Delicately, carefully, he eased it out. It was very large. Bloody matter poured from the cut. He took two stitches to close it and applied the matted hair to stanch the flow of blood. "Esteban, tell the man he will be well and free of pain."

The Indians had watched the operation. After Esteban announced the patient would get well, one of his brothers spoke. "Sacred Ones. Children of the Sun. You, to whom your great father reveals everything; you, from whom nothing can remain hidden; you have supreme power. Our most powerful medicine men have tried to suck out the evil from my brother's chest. The pebbles they spat out did not cure him. You had but to put your hand inside and pluck the offending arrowhead out. All of us have watched this wonder. All of us have touched and felt what you removed. We shall send it to our neighbours who live in the mountains, and tell them that the Children of the Sun are here. They will come to join us when we sing and dance to honour you."

Hundreds of Indians converged on that encampment and watched when, two days later, Vaca cut the stitches. The patient moved his arm gently to show he was free of pain; he let them look at his scar, as thin and fine as a crease in the palm of his hand.

Vaca's spectacular and successful operation testified to the truth of the myth whose origin he had derided. Their divinity, thus established, became potent and indestructible. People from many groups wanted to live in the company of the Children of the Sun; a vibrant faith brought separate groups together into a community larger than any had known before. An ever-lengthening procession snaked across the land, over mountain ridges and grassy plains and down lovely watered valleys. Numbering thousands of marchers, the procession, like a rainbow bright with the colours of human hopes, stretched from horizon to horizon and proclaimed the existence of a world free from death and woe.

There was order and organization on the march. The men, as was the custom, hunted. There were those who hunted only rabbits—each man carried a club three palms long. When a rabbit jumped—and the countryside teemed with them—they threw the clubs with such dexterity and precision that they forced it to jump into waiting hands. Other hunters were armed with bows and arrows; they scattered away from the line of march in pursuit of deer and other game. Leaving the men free to hunt, the women transported everything including the extra mats for their buhíos—each of the four Children of the Sun had his own—and as they walked, they collected a harvest of prickly pears, spiders, worms, and whatever else their sharp eyes found.

When twilight fell, the hunters brought their game to the Children of the Sun. Before each, five or six deer, many quail and eight or ten backloads of rabbits were piled up. The women too brought what they had garnered. Everything was blessed—until that was done, no Indian

would touch anything. After this first blessing, the game was roasted in dozens of specially prepared ovens. From each oven, the Children of the Sun took a small token piece, giving the rest to be divided among the groups. Then came the second blessing. The three or four thousand marchers passed in single file before the Children of the Sun to have them breathe upon and bless their food.

"Have so many ever come together before?" Esteban said, looking at the multitude camped around them.

"How long can it continue?" Dorantes, too, wondered. "Already game is getting short."

"I am grateful they only ask us to bless their food and do not expect us to provide game for the hunters." And Castillo added, "I felt better when there were not so many."

"That may happen sooner than you think," Vaca said. "I think some have already turned back. They must know that in the mountains ahead food will be scarce."

"That explains why last night after the second blessing two large groups thanked us and promised never to forget," Esteban said. "It was their goodbye. Tonight I noticed they were not waiting to be blessed. They must have started back for their own territory."

The procession shrank as it advanced across the cordilleras, parallel chains of rugged mountains; the hunters brought in fewer deer, quail, and rabbits. Sensitive to the diminishing amount of food, the Indians became apprehensive and undecided. Dare they continue? They knew that starvation was the price they would pay for overtaxing the region's resources. Each day more turned back.

"They are melting away as quickly as ice does under a hot sun," Dorantes said a few days later. "I hope we shall not lose our entire escort before we find the next group."

"I was marvelling at the orderliness of their withdrawal," Vaca answered. "Am I right in thinking that they are turning back in the same order in which they joined us?"

Esteban said, "Don Álvar, soon we will know if you are right. From thousands to hundreds—it is hard to tell. We shall see which group remains last. I remember which was the last to join."

The procession had dwindled back to an escorting group, the last to join, with whom they finally crossed the next-to-the-last ridge. They were welcomed by new hosts who, whether because news of the size of the procession had reached them or they had been told of the great giveaway expected of them, brought more goods than the escort could carry away. After their escort had taken all they could, Esteban saw heaps of gifts left untouched and suggested to their hosts that they take them back. "A man would be without honour to take back gifts he has given," an Indian asserted sadly but with pride. Custom forbade it, so on the side of the mountain where the meeting had taken place, the presents remained unclaimed, unwanted. This tribe, so fervent in their faith, so true to tradition, was the one that suddenly, dramatically brought the four to the edge of disaster.

No one expected terrifying consequences when, in his routine way, Esteban announced that the Children of the Sun desired to go where the sun sets. The Indians' first response was a reluctance to escort the four. They said the next group was too distant. Esteban persevered and urged them to send messengers announcing their approach. Again they demurred; they offered excuses. After much pressing, they confessed that the group to the west were their ancient enemies, with whom they warred and feuded.

Castillo and Dorantes thought the Indians were shilly-shallying; Vaca thought it more serious—either they were lazy or disobedient; Esteban was not certain—he heard a note of despair in their voices when they spoke to him. He continued to press, and at last they sent two women to find the group to the west, since women can negotiate even during a war. One woman was of their tribe, the other had been captured as a girl from the enemy group. A week passed and they did not return. The Indians' statement that the women had probably not been able to locate anyone sounded like more excuses. And when the four suggested that the Indians escort them to the north instead, the response was the same: reluctance and excuses. Days passed and nothing happened.

"We must act," Vaca said to the others. "Summer is passing. The harvest moon was new when we arrived; it is now waning. Their stubbornness is serious. We cannot go on easily without them, and they are too afraid of their enemies to take us. I have been thinking that perhaps fear of their gods might be stronger than fear of their enemies. We must show them we are serious in our request. Maybe we can prod them to act. I shall put up my buhío in the woods apart from the encampment. And as I, so you remain aloof also."

"The Children of the Sun are angry." The terrible news

was whispered. "The gods are offended." Fear, like a plague, swept through the encampment.

Stricken, the Indians crawled to Vaca's buhío, remained sleepless, pitifully moaning as though in pain; mouthing their fears; helpless. They beseeched him to hold his anger, they pleaded, they promised to lead the Children of the Sun in whatever direction they desired. They would even go outside their territory, though they knew that they would die when they did. They were ready to step off the edge of their world into nothingness if the gods asked it.

Their words were meaningless to Vaca, but he had no need to understand their prayers to know their anguish. Acting as he thought proper in the face of what seemed simple obstinacy, and lest the Indians' fears should lift too quickly and easily, he stayed within his buhío, continuing to act displeased. While the four were intent on their own stratagem, a shocking and dreadful thing came to pass. By twos and threes men fell senseless to the ground, writhing, then motionless.

Their parents and brothers and wives tried to rouse them. Of the number who were so afflicted, eight died the same day. The arrow of the wilderness, large with Indian hopes, pointed with the myth of their belief, barbed with their fear, had struck. No longer could the Children of the Sun remain apart and aloof.

"We have sinned. We have killed them," Vaca cried out at the tragedy that overwhelmed them as well as the Indians. "We underestimated the power of their faith. Could anyone have thought that fear would kill? It is as though we had shot them. Forgive us. We must stop this at once. Esteban, tell us, what are they saying?"

"They are saying the same thing over and over again. 'Unless you forgive us, we are all doomed. We beg you to give up your anger. Do not insist that more men die. Already too many have died because you willed it. Give up your anger against us.' " So Esteban translated. "Don Álvar, their explanation is that we caused these eight men to die to satisfy our anger. They are spreading word of this to all who live nearby. What shall I tell them?"

It was the turn of the Children of the Sun to taste of fear. What, each thought in his heart, if Our Lord is punishing us. Have we encouraged the Indians to worship idols? The old doubts nagged at them. Is God testing us?

"If this morbid fear kills our hosts," Vaca reviewed the grave situation and the serious predicament they were threatened with, "if the Indians slip away to find safety, if they infect their neighbours with the same killing malady." He looked long and hard at the other three. "Andrés, Esteban, Alonso, I am full of ifs: if, if . . . you, too, are uncertain. There is only one help. Let us pray to Our Lord. The fate of the Indians and our fate is in His hands. Only He can save us all."

They knelt and prayed earnestly, bringing the fear out of their hearts. They prayed long, and ease of spirit came. The Indians watching their quiet devotions felt relieved; they were reassured to see the celestial visitors speaking gently to their father, the sun. Almost as quickly as they had sickened, the ill began to get well.

"How fragile, how exceedingly fragile is spiritual

health," Vaca said. "God alone holds the delicate balance between life and death." The near disaster made the four aware that they would never again do anything that might bring tragedy to people whose qualities they had learned to esteem. "They are kind and generous, well-conditioned and honest. Our artifice was not worthy of their nature."

The group was on its way to full recovery by the time the two women scouts finally returned. They reported having great difficulty locating any people, it being the fall, the season when the Indians moved about the plains on their annual hunt. The next morning the four, accompanied by the most robust men and women, started westward. After a few days they camped while Alonso and Esteban walked ahead guided by the two women. The captured woman led them to a height above a great river that flowed between steep cliffs; below, not too distant, was the town where her father lived. The two men saw a cheering sight: houses sturdily built and permanent.

The houses were a clear sign that some sort of boundary had been crossed. The Indians they were about to meet were different from the hunting, food-gathering groups with whom they had been wandering. "I remember," Esteban said to Alonso as they looked down on this heartening sight, "the excitement of the men who led the caravans across the Sahara when they sighted a town. And how different the caravan merchants were from those of the bazaars. Both were merchants, but they thought and acted very differently. Why should we have thought that all the Indians would be like those we have lived with so far?"

"A pleasant sight," Castillo kept repeating. "I am not a snail—I like houses that are not carried about."

After a brief welcome and look around the town, Esteban stayed on to gain a little familiarity with the language while Castillo with the two women and five or six of the new group went back to where the main party awaited them.

"Don Álvar," Castillo burst out excitedly as soon as they met, "we are on our way to Mexico. I am sure of it. The new people have permanent houses—solid stone. Also they grow beans and squash. Their gardens remind me of Aute." He ended in a climax of joy: "Maize, they have maize!"

The three with their large escort were still a distance from the town when they were met by Esteban and the townspeople. On a rocky height of land, the two groups, bitter, ancient, and implacable enemies, met. It was the first time in the memory of anyone there that they had met in peace. They looked at each other, but could not converse since their languages were utterly different. The woman who had been captured left her husband's group and joined that of her father. When that living link had been made, the two groups, through the Children of the Sun, performed the giveaway: pumpkins, beautifully tanned leather skins, and other offerings were given to those who had served as escorts. Memory of the meeting would stay long with the two groups.

"The border we crossed," Vaca said that night, when they were pleasantly lodged in the town, "was not marked, nor noteworthy in any detail. To us it was invisible. Yet it exists. The mere thought of crossing it peacefully killed eight men. If they had not died, we never would have known that we were leaving one nation for another."

THE CHILDREN OF THE SUN called them the "Cow Nation" because the name bison, or, as the animals were to be called later, buffaloes, was not known. They were the very first men of the Old World to see the heavy-headed lords of the great plains, whose herds darkly patterned the immense sea of grass. Noble in appearance, the buffaloes waxed large and fat and multiplied vastly. Those who hunted them, the Cow People, were, the four decided, the finest of any group they had encountered: handsome, active, and strong, they were, from their manner of answering questions, also the most alert.

Food was available in abundance—but how did puny men hunt such huge beasts? That was the first question asked when later the four sat conversing with an impressive group of men. Like the other Indians, they wore only a loincloth, though some of the older men had deerskin shirts. Esteban relayed the questions and the answers as given.

"How do they hunt the cows?" Dorantes began. "No matter how strong and fast, how can men manage to kill such formidable beasts without arquebuses, and on foot?"

"Sometimes two or three hunt alone," the answer came. "A few hunters do not frighten the herd; their eyesight is weak and they do not notice two or three who creep close, each covered with a cowhide. The wind must be blowing away from the animals—their sense of smell is good. Arrows in the exact place bring the animal down. If one becomes aroused and charges, we still have the lance." And the warrior fingered a flint-tipped weapon that lay by his side.

Said another, "The usual way is the Big Hunt. All join together when the scouts sight a herd. They tell the Chief of the Hunt; he directs everything and gives the signal so all start together. Sometimes he has us drive the cows to where men with arrows are waiting. Sometimes, if the herd is very large, we stampede them so they rush over the cliffs. Men with lances finish them off."

"Whatever method is used," Dorantes commented after hearing this, "to hunt such powerful animals on foot with nothing better than arrows and lances demands great courage and the discipline of a cavalry corps."

"Can you imagine the success we would have if we hunted them on horses and had muskets?" Castillo asked. "But if they kill a herd in one engagement, wouldn't the meat get rotten? They have no pepper or other spices. How do they keep it?"

To answer that, a man told a woman to bring long, thin strips of meat, brown and hard. "The meat is cut so and dried in the sun. It will keep all winter." The woman said something. "She has some already pounded into a powder. Go with her. She will show you what a fine food it makes when cooked in water."

Castillo went to look. After a few minutes he came back for the others. "Come—you must see their strange way of cooking. They boil even though they have no pots they can put on the fire. Extraordinary. Remarkable. What ingenuity. Come and see." And the four watched the woman throwing fire-heated stones into a calabash half-filled with water. Handling the hot stones with twigs, she kept adding them until the water boiled. Then she took a handful of brown powder from a leather pouch and threw it into the pot. After that, she continued adding hot stones and fishing out the cooled ones until she was satisfied the soup was cooked. They all agreed that it took great skill to handle the stones and to cook without fire.

Vaca then wanted to know why, if the Indians planted beans and pumpkins, they did not grow maize.

"If we had planted maize, we would have lost all we put into the ground. There has been no rain for two years. Last year moles ate the seed we planted. Until we have rain, good rain, we dare not risk losing more. Sacred Ones," the speaker addressed the Children of the Sun, "we need rain. Tell the sky to rain."

"We shall pray for rain so that you may plant your maize," Esteban assured them.

"Ask him," Vaca continued, "where the maize we have seen comes from. If they lost all they planted, they must be getting new supplies from somewhere."

The Indian answered by pointing toward the setting sun. "We go to the people who live in that direction. In that country it grows in all settlements. The best path, the one we take, is up the river. It is circuitous but there is food to be had along the way."

"First you go north and then west? Is there a more direct path to the maize country?" Esteban asked.

"If you go straight toward the setting sun, you will

reach it after seventeen days. The path is straight, but you will find only *chacan* to keep from starving. Chacan will keep you alive, but it is bad—dry and bitter and hard to swallow. Try some and you will see I speak the truth." And the four tasted a powder offered to them. Indeed, as the Indian said, it was impossible to swallow.

They stayed with the Cow People two days, trying to decide whether to take the roundabout path that first led northward, or strike directly to the west.

"In my opinion," Vaca said, "we should take the route to the west. I hold it certain that going toward the sunset we must find what we desire."

Where the trails forked, the Children of the Sun took that to the west. They had asked for and received, each one, a bag filled with tallow, and had the Indians sent to guide them similarly provided for. They had learned from earlier groups that a handful eaten at night would sustain them for the day's march.

Seventeen grim days across the desert they would march, and then another seventeen days across the continental divide.

From the ridge overlooking the first settled villages, they saw green gardens. Behind them lay the harsh, dry region they had traversed. The valley below was bright with farms. The Indians they met offered them quantities of maize—both in the grain and flour—beans and pumpkins, cotton blankets; everything the people had, they offered.

As was their custom, the Children of the Sun kept nothing but gave all to the Cow People guides, thanking God for having brought them safely through the empty wilderness into the land of plenty.

"Thus the Children of the Sun receive from one and give to the others," said one of the grateful Cow People guides to the Indian elders who had looked on. "Those who brought them to us spoke of their great power. You have seen that they are good—trust them. Their ceremonies will bring you health and peace." These words, solemnly spoken, made their path southward delightful all the way. A succession of villages greeted them and provided them with offerings and escorts.

"Did I ever tell you about the travelling acrobats who used to visit Azamor?" Esteban said one night, after they had enjoyed their daily meal. The sense of well-being and comradeship took him back to his childhood. "One of their tricks was climbing a greased pole. We tried but we could not get up far. I remember how easy it was to slide down. I keep feeling we are sliding down the greased pole."

"And I," Dorantes said, "have been remembering how my horse, after an all-day, cross-country ride, would suddenly step forward, briskly toss his head and swish his tail, knowing that hay and water and rest were near at hand."

"I wish I had my lute," Castillo said suddenly. "I would make music such as Orpheus made, songs of sorrow and sweetness, to tell that we have come back from hades."

"Where is hades?" Esteban asked innocently.

"Hades was the word the ancient Romans used for

hell, the place without hope. After our long years of slavery, this is being alive. Don't you feel it is so, Don Álvar?"

"I am filled with the wonder of God's goodness to us. Every day the promise of being reunited with the Christians comes closer to fulfillment. These gentle, good people have started a new procession and despite the time we spend blessing them it is gathering speed. But," he added lightly, "I cannot sing like Orpheus, I can only join you in sliding down a greased pole and you in neighing like a homing horse."

The Indians' insistence on being touched and blessed by the Children of the Sun was demanding. When a woman in the procession gave birth, she would bring the new-born infant to be blessed. All Indians held full faith that the four came from heaven, a belief carefully fostered by their behaviour. Though they walked all day, they ate only one meal, a meagre one at night; and to safeguard their influence and authority, they continued their custom of communicating with the Indians through Esteban. He was called He-Who-Speaks-for-the-Children of the Sun.

Because the ceremony of the Indians of one group escorting the four to the next persisted, and because the procession passed through the territories of tribes who were enemies, the ceremony of the giveaway forced friendship on them. And so warfare ceased throughout that region and there was peace. Here, thought Vaca, are people of good character and nature, capable of learning and of changing. Perhaps God intended for us to bring them peace, perhaps even the blessing of speaking of Him.

Vaca addressed them through Esteban. "In heaven there is a Man whom we call God. He created the sky and the earth. Him we worship. From Him comes all good. Do as we do and all will go well." And then he made the sign of the cross.

The Indians thought it right and proper for the Children to speak thus of their father, the sun. They began a strange ceremony designed to carry out the commandment they had been given and increase the blessings they received. At sunrise and again at sunset they raised their arms to the sky and then as though they held some precious essence in their cupped hands they anointed their bodies with it. After that they made the sign of the cross.

And so they came to the settlement they called the Town of the Deer Hearts, because its inhabitants presented Dorantes with a most unusual offering. "There must be five or six hundred," Dorantes estimated, amazed at the large pile of deer hearts offered. Here, too, they received arrowheads, beautifully carved out of green stone, honoured in their most sacred songs and dances.

"The stones look bright and clear. Could they be emeralds?" Vaca asked, looking closely at the splendid gifts. "Where do they find them?"

"They are found," Esteban was told in answer to his question, "in the north. On the top of one of the four sacred mountains. Close by are towns with many, many inhabitants. Their houses are larger and better built than ours. To get these, we gave a great number of fine parrot plumes and feathers."

"And this? Where does this come from?" Esteban held up some beads of coral.

"From the great salt water to the west," they answered. "Between is poor country that takes us fifteen marches to cross."

They stayed in the Town of the Deer Hearts for three days and Dorantes went out with the hunters to see how they could secure such great numbers of deer.

"Do you remember how we used to have to run all day to tire out one poor half-starved deer? Here they only have to wound an animal." Dorantes was describing his experience. "There is a certain tree, small, very green and pleasing. Its fruit, a little smaller than an apple, has a poison so deadly that the merest scratch kills. All they have to do is moisten their arrows with it and—one, two, three, finish."

While being escorted to the next village, they thought about all the unusual things they had seen at the Town of the Deer Hearts, especially what the coral and turquoise and emeralds might signify. At the end of the day's march, the procession was stopped. It was forced to wait until a river, swollen by recent rains to a swirling, brown torrent, subsided. A fortnight passed in inaction. One afternoon, Castillo noticed an Indian wearing what looked to him like a locket made out of a sword belt buckle with the nail of a horseshoe stitched to it. Quickly he sought Esteban.

"Wearing an amulet?" Esteban asked Castillo, as together they sought the Indian. "So far I haven't noticed anyone wearing an amulet. Of course, in Azamor everyone wore one. I did."

When they examined what the Indian wore, it was exactly what Castillo had thought. "Where do these things come from?" Esteban asked the Indian, fingering the buckle and nail. A small group quickly collected.

"From heaven," the answer came, serious and straight.

"But who brought them?"

"Some men from heaven came to the river. They had hair like yours." He pointed to Castillo's beard. "They had horses and long thick knives tied to their waists," the owner of the amulet said.

"And lances," added another Indian. "They killed two Indians. They put their lances into the water; then they got into the water; and finally we saw them moving on the surface toward the setting sun."

Not quite certain exactly what the Indians meant, Esteban and Castillo did not try to question further but rejoined the other two who were impatiently waiting.

"There is absolutely no question, Don Álvar. There are Spaniards on the other side of that river." Castillo spoke slowly. They were quiet as they let the meaning of the words take hold. There was nothing to say; their impossible hope had come true. They tasted the joy of their long-cherished desire to be reunited with their countrymen; they were humbly thankful for God's compassion and His grace, so steadfastly vouchsafed to them. But the thought of the killing haunted them.

After a while Dorantes voiced what they all feared. "Could they be slave-catchers . . . ?"

Helplessly they waited, looking at the boiling river that barred their way, the wide muddy ditch through which dirty rainwater poured wildly. Forced to wait, they waited, their impatience slowly seasoned with anger against Spaniards who were wantonly killing *their* Indians, impaling them on their lances as though they were sticking wild pigs. The joy of their triumphant reunion changed as they accepted the reality of what they had accomplished and what remained to be done.

Caught between feelings of bright exaltation and sombre outrage they waited for the flood to abate.

S LAVE-CATCHERS . . . A week after the four had crossed the river with the procession, Indians guided the Children of the Sun up a steep, hidden trail to a town that clung to the edge of a mountain. It was jammed with refugees. There, the four heard of men and women caught and tied, driven helpless before monsters who prodded them with long, sharp knives. Everywhere were children, lost without their parents, hungry, bewildered. Every day, every hour, brought new evidence of atrocities committed by their countrymen.

Hasten, hasten, Children of the Sun. *Hasten*. Find the savages who perpetrated the crimes. *Hasten, hasten*. Command them: You shall not kill; you shall not enslave; you shall not violate families and homes, nor wound, maim nor visit outrages upon human beings. *Speed, speed*—the empty, ravaged countryside cried out. *Faster, faster*—urged the burnt villages and their inhabitants, homeless, weak, and thin, hiding by day and gnawing on roots and the bark of trees at night.

Weep for a fertile and beautiful land where villages had taken root and where now the only living things were bands of vultures heavy with their ghastly feasting on corpses, too heavy to fly away from the marching procession, too satiated to finish and leave bones picked clean and dry. Comfort and bless the survivors, starving, apathetic, longing for death. Weep, weep, weep for the misery and hunger and death brought by greedy, godless men.

A righteous anger burned fiercely in the hearts of the Children of the Sun as the sound of agony rose in a terrible dirge endlessly repeated. Men riding horses had appeared and senselessly destroyed and looted and burned; they had herded up the able-bodied men, the women and children and driven them off as captives. Christians, Spaniards. A brutal, bitter reunion. Catastrophe lay at the end of their long quest. Christians, Spaniards. The unbearable shame that they too had once believed that superiority was a matter of being clothed and armed and mounted.

Hasten, hasten; speed, speed; faster, faster.

Leaving Castillo and Dorantes to protect the Indians and follow at the procession's pace, Vaca and Esteban went swiftly forward, with eleven Indians as guides and trackers, to make contact with the Spaniards. A day and a half later, swinging along the foothills, they caught sight of horsemen. The two groups saw each other at a distance. The mounted soldiers—Vaca and Esteban counted four—reined in their horses and looked. A body of Indians coming toward them! Never had it happened before. As the party approached swiftly, the Spaniards could make out among the naked Indians, and just as naked, a bearded man with long blond hair, and a black man. Dumbfounded, they sat, neither speaking nor moving. Was the light, the sun, playing tricks? They rubbed their eyes and kept looking. The party did not shout to them. When they were close enough to speak, the blond savage stepped forward and spoke in Spanish.

"Who is in charge of your company?"

"Captain Diego de Alcaraz, sir. He is camped a few miles from here."

"I will talk with him. Lead the way." Without further exchange, horsemen and naked foot party went together.

Like his men, Alcaraz was speechless at the sight of the approaching party. Was that an albino, he thought, remembering the albino jester of His Catholic Majesty, Charles V; but he was a hunchback. As these thoughts raced through his mind, the blond man came to meet him.

"I am Álvar Núñez Cabeza de Vaca, Treasurer and High-Sheriff of La Florida, under the grant given Governor Pánfilo de Narváez."

"Captain Diego de Alcaraz, at your orders. But," and he spluttered, "but—the Narváez expedition was a long time ago. Was it eight? no; nine? no. Ten years. We thought them all dead."

"Not all. Four are alive. Esteban who is with me and the Captains Alonso Castillo de Maldonado and Andrés Dorantes de Carranca." Listening to Vaca, Esteban was suddenly aware that his name was as naked as his body.

"And the others?" Alcaraz asked.

"Permit me first to complete the formalities. Be kind enough to have a certificate drawn up for me stating the year, month, and day of my arrival and the manner of my coming."

Ah! these Spanish, Esteban thought, marvelling at

Vaca's words. How firmly committed they are to notaries and certificates and lists. Don Álvar is wise; he knows that without papers he could remain lost, missing. A certificate and not his living body is the only reality of existence the administrators recognize.

"But Don Álvar," Alcaraz persisted, "forgive me if I do not seem able to understand. Narváez sailed to La Florida, which is washed by the Atlantic Ocean, and you come out of the wilderness north of Culiacán, on the Pacific side of Mexico. How?" His mind was dizzy thinking how impossible it was.

"Not now, Captain. You will hear everything. But a little later. The story will keep. Tell me how your venture is going? That is the important thing now." Vaca kept his voice affable, bland. He wanted to know something about the man with whom he would be dealing. It was part of his nature to assess his opponent.

Alcaraz seemed to need only Vaca's inquiry to pour out his troubles; it was as though Vaca had reappeared after his long sojourn in the wilderness for the express purpose of helping the Captain out of his troubles. Weeks had passed, the captain explained, since his men had found any Indians to capture; he did not know in which direction to search; and worst of all, his men were beginning to grumble that they were hungry and tired.

Listening to the captain's petty complaints and unsatisfied greed, Vaca knew he was dealing with a vicious, weak man: poor stuff. He also knew how greatly the four had changed during their years of questing. There was no way he could keep Dorantes and Castillo back, nor stop the procession from coming into the clutches of Alcaraz.

His greatest concern was to protect the Indians who were following the Children of the Sun. The wilderness was still with Vaca.

He sent Esteban with three horsemen to meet the procession, charging him to alert Dorantes and Castillo to the slave-catchers' machinations, and guide them to Alcaraz's camp. And though Vaca had told him, Alcaraz could not believe the sight he saw—a multitude of Indians, for the procession had been swollen by additional hundreds who left their hiding places to find safety with the Children of the Sun. His face lit up with greed and the joy he felt at the mere thought of the fortune he would make from his share of such a wholesale enslavement. His worries were over: not only were there Indians, they brought food. The astonished Spaniards watched the Indians offer the Children of the Sun containers filled with maize which they had sealed and buried to keep from the marauders.

That evening Esteban joined the other three. He had been walking near the soldiers; he was disturbed, angry. "I have just heard the most shameful words. These pigs and sons of pigs who are eating the Indians' maize are laughing and planning how to enslave them. They say we are simpletons and fools, and if we don't put on clothes, they'll sell us, too."

"Lord, Lord," Vaca said, his voice matching Esteban's in anger and outrage. "I have been wondering how You can permit men like that to live. They make me ashamed to be a Spaniard. I knew Alcaraz thought we had been made foolish by our long association with the Indians. We have been away from civilization too long," he said bitterly, adding, "I shall do everything I can to upset his plans. But I know that here on the frontier, he is more than a match for me. I shall do what I can. But I have sworn that if I fail here I shall not fail when I meet whoever is supreme in Mexico City."

Vaca also was confronted with another problem, very different, but also very pressing. Esteban had been telling them, "The Indians will not steal away and return to their homes or go into hiding. They tell me that it is their sacred duty to escort us to other Indians. It is the proper ceremony; it is the custom. They are convinced that if they fail to do this, they will all die. Don Álvar, the procession, with all its ceremonies, must come to an end. But how?"

"We urged the Indians who came out of hiding not to join us," Dorantes said.

"They are convinced that when they are with us, neither the Christians or their lances can harm them," Castillo added. "Christians are demons like Bad Thing. We are Children of the Sun. Very different."

"It was they who made us Children of the Sun," Esteban said. "We must arrange for them to unmake us."

"And the myth? A myth, our professor used to say, cannot be killed," Castillo warned. "The Children of the Sun will live, no matter what we do."

"Then, Don Álvar," Esteban said, "we must invent a ceremony. Suppose you speak to them, not through me; suppose you distribute maize, not through Alonso and Andrés, but directly; they will obey. In all their talk, you are Older Brother, to whom we listen."

They were caught between the rapacity and cruelty

of Alcaraz and the Indians' firm devotion. How to prevent
the one and end the other honourably and decently. Unable to sleep, they talked far into the night. From a Narváez to an Alcaraz! They began to feel that the wilderness
between had been a Garden of Eden where they had
walked under the protection of God, daily knowing Him
and His grace. Though they had made their re-entry into
the world, the wilderness was still with them.

Thinking to stop this nonsense of the legend of the
Children of the Sun—he was irked by Vaca's superior
airs and eager to harvest a fortune in slaves—Alcaraz
addressed the Indians through his interpreter when they
had gathered for their daily blessing. Bluntly, he said the
four were fakes. They were not Children of the Sun but
Christians and Spaniards; four poor, helpless men who had
been lost and had wandered a long time. He, Alcaraz, on
the other hand, was lord of the land and must be obeyed
and served. The Indians listened quietly. They discussed
what they had been told, conversing among themselves.
Then one, acting as their spokesman, gave their answer
to Alcaraz. "You do not speak the truth. The Children
of the Sun came from where the sun rises; you from
where it sets. The Children of the Sun heal the sick; you
kill those of sound health. The Children of the Sun came
naked and barefoot; you are clothed, ride horses, and carry
lances. The Children of the Sun took nothing for themselves and gave away everything offered them; you give
nothing and rob us of everything, even our freedom."
When the four heard this, they knew that Alcaraz had
provided them with the moment to end the procession.

Standing with the other three, Vaca spoke to the Indians in a ceremony of farewell. He urged them to return in peace to their villages, to rebuild their houses, to plant and cultivate their gardens. When he had finished talking, for the last time each person was touched and blessed by the Children of the Sun.

They did not know that crossing the boundary between the wilderness and New Spain would be marked by death.

Lost in the slave-catching jungle of Alcaraz just as they emerged from the wilderness, they were rescued by Captain Melchior Diaz, in charge of Culiacán, the northwesternmost frontier settlement. A hard, tough man, he knew better than to maltreat a nobleman like Vaca—his position as treasurer of La Florida showed he had the king's favour, and his being alive proved he had God's as well. Whatever the dangers of the frontier, Diaz counted them less deadly than the backbiting, malice, and jealousy of the capital. More than once he himself had said that so-and-so had had his head cut off and never knew it until, poor man, he tried to turn it. When Diaz received news of the survivors' appearance, he was grateful to play a little part in so great a miracle. Rushing out to meet them, he wept tears of pity and joy at the sight of the four, and thanked God that He had preserved them during their lengthy ordeal.

"Everything I have, anything I can command, is yours, Don Álvar Núñez," he said. His words, the homecoming welcome the four had dreamed of, meant nothing, for they learned that unknown to them, Alcaraz had ordered some of his men to follow the Indians as they had obediently made their way homeward; most of them had been caught and enslaved. The great procession, dedicated to the Children of the Sun, had been wilfully and wantonly transformed into a march into slavery.

Fifteen days later they were ready to leave Culiacán for Mexico City. Vaca and Diaz had arranged a contract that satisfied the deepest hopes of both men: Diaz wanted to restore the ravaged province, to establish peace and make the region productive again. Vaca insisted that Alcaraz's raids be stopped. While the Children of the Sun could not free those already enslaved, nor bring back those who had died, nor heal those who had been maimed, they could witness the solemn, sacred pledge signed by Diaz in which he promised that Spaniards would not invade the villages of the Indians or enslave any who accepted Christianity. Not now or ever.

When this had been arranged, the Children of the Sun summoned all the Indians from far and near to come to them so that they might speak their farewell, their absolutely final farewell. Firm in their devotion, the Indians gathered.

He-Who-Speaks-for-the-Children of the Sun addressed the Indians for the last time. "Have no fear. Leave your mountain hiding places in confidence. Peace has come. Return to your own lands and rebuild your villages. When you erect your houses, erect one for God. Place a cross over the door. From this time on, when Christians come among you, meet them with crosses in your hands, not bows and arrows. Give them food to eat and a place to sleep. They will not harm you. They will be your friends."

Then the four moved among the multitude of Indians,

touching and blessing each one; finally, in unison they made the sign of the cross over them all.

All this took place before a notary and in the presence of witnesses; so it was written down and signed.

The next day, May 15, 1536, they left Culiacán for Mexico City.

I⸻T WAS HARD shedding the wilderness. They had to readjust in little ways and big ways. There was the time in Compostella where they met Nuño de Guzmán, governor of the province and at the height of his career. No one could have been more generous and sympathetic, more helpful and charming. He fitted them out from his own wardrobe and provided fine beds for their rest. But the clothes oppressed them, and when they lay down in the beds, they tossed and turned, unable to get comfortable. They thanked the governor for his kindness; in their own room they took off the clothes and slept on the ground.

"It is not only that they are uncomfortable," Dorantes said, drawing his cotton blanket around his shoulders and looking at the clothes he had taken off. "They smell. I had forgotten the smell of stale sweat."

"And how clothes hold it," Castillo added. "That's how the Indians of La Florida knew when Narváez was approaching. They could smell us coming."

"In Azamor, it used to be said that Nazarenes bathe only once in their lives—when they are baptized," Esteban said, and they all laughed.

"It took time to learn to feel at ease without clothes,"

Vaca commented. "By the time we reach Mexico City we shall be accustomed. Our noses, too. But the beds— that is a private matter and I shall continue to prefer the floor."

As when they had moved forward with the procession, so now news of their incredible homecoming travelled ahead of them as they rode toward Mexico City. Men and women stood to see them pass. In Guadalajara, the town Guzmán founded and named for his hometown in Spain, a young man, his pitted face tanned deeply by the sun, came up to Vaca.

"Don Álvar Núñez, do you remember me?" His eyes were bright as he asked. "Simon de Cuenca, at your orders. I served under you against the French in Navarre. You may not remember me because I did poorly; I suffered much from boils. Here, God be praised, I am well. God be doubly praised that I see you again. This is the greatest day of my life."

"So you were one of those useless ones that had boils," Vaca said, and the two men smiled at each other and spoke briefly of old times. And then, at much greater length of new times, of New Spain and the changes taking place.

Cuenca sounded the first warning. "Don't be too enthusiastic about Guzmán's generosity. You couldn't know that of *all* the slavers he is the most brutal and most successful. That should be enough for you. It's common talk that he will be broken very soon. Not for that. He is capable; also imprudent. He has made bitter enemies of the viceroy and Cortés, the two most powerful men in New Spain. Take care, Don Álvar Núñez."

Vaca thanked him. "We shall be guided by what you have told us. We shall be discreet; have no fear. Tell me, who is the viceroy? When did he arrive?"

"Don Antonio de Mendoza. He arrived but recently. People speak well of him."

"Don Antonio de Mendoza," Vaca repeated the name slowly. "He is probably of the cardinal's family; in the time of Ferdinand and Isabella he was called the Third Monarch. And Cortés? How goes Don Hernando? After all, we have a bond in common: Narváez," Vaca said with a grim smile.

"He is now the Marquess del Valle. His Majesty loaded him with honours and a fine title. He was given immense properties—the whole valley of Oaxaca. But he still calls himself Cortés."

"What title can match the lustre of his name?" Vaca asked. And then, as the full meaning of his question became clear, he added thoughtfully, "except viceroy."

That night, when the four were eating together, Vaca discussed what was on his mind. "How simple things were in the wilderness, where we could set our course by the setting sun. When there are two suns, Mendoza and Cortés, it is harder to know what direction to take. Which will win? Courtier or conquistador?"

"You make it sound like a bullfight," Castillo remarked, interested in the thought of rivalry at the topmost level.

"Not a bullfight, Alonso," Vaca said, amused at Castillo's figure of speech. "Not a bullfight at all. As we say in Estramadura: When there are two bulls in the ring, no bullfight is possible."

In triumph they rode to Mexico City. The wonder of
their return, a reunion after ten years' questing, was
renewed at each of the many Spanish settlements they
passed through on their ride. Never had there been such
heroes. Word of their approach went ahead of them, and
wine and cakes offered to them on their arrival made their
ride the occasion for a continuous holiday. They had
cheated death; people gathered to see and marvel, to shout
welcome and well-done, God be praised and Godspeed.
Looking at them, people were reminded of miracles, of
Lazarus raised from the dead and restored to his family.

Nine hundred miles from Culiacán to Mexico City—
and before that how many thousands had they walked
since escaping from slavery? Like a wave that gathers
force and shape as it moves toward the shore, so the
return of the castaways, begun desperately, far away, long
ago, gained meaning and momentum until, their quest attained, they rode into the capital of New Spain where,
standing side by side, Mendoza and Cortés, viceroy and
conqueror, gave them a joyous, royal welcome.

The time was early evening. The bells of all the churches
and convents rang the hour of vespers; the day, Sunday;
the date, July 24, 1536, eve of the national fiesta of Santiago, Saint James the apostle. To all pious people, their arrival on the eve of that glorious celebration was a sure
sign that the Blessed Apostle himself had looked after
them. How else was it possible that they had returned
from their long and arduous journey in the wilderness?

5 / How the Quest Ended

"Is this heaven or home?" Castillo asked half-seriously, half-jokingly. "It must be home because being a Child of the Sun did not prepare me." And he looked around him in wonder. "Or is home heaven?"

They were the viceroy's guests, lodged in his palace. It was truly splendid, the furnishings sumptuous and costly; yet it was not fully regal, being a miniature of the king's residence. Scores of Indian servants, dressed in spotless white, served the viceroy, his retainers, and guests; some thirty gentlemen attended him, forming his mounted escort when he rode out. Luxury and silken elegance had replaced the conquistadors' garb, announcing plainly that the day of the swashbuckling fortune hunter was over.

Though recently arrived in Mexico City, Don Antonio de Mendoza had already imposed on the colonial capital the style and formal stateliness of the Spanish court. As the first viceroy, he was expected to establish the royal authority in New Spain. It was a frontier, a fabulously rich, imperial frontier that extended from the Isthmus, which Balboa had won, through the Aztec empire which Cortés had conquered, to the northwestern province recently carved out by Guzmán. Still young, the capable

Don Antonio was both ambitious and cautious: ambitious to discover for his king lands richer and kingdoms more golden than Mexico; cautious lest any probings beyond the frontier offend Cortés, already hurt that he had not been named viceroy, and infringe on the conqueror's rights to explore northward.

To Vaca and his three companions, Don Antonio was the perfect host—gracious, generous, never intrusive, always interested. For several weeks they stayed in the palace writing the account of their wanderings while they were still together and the myriad details were still fresh in their minds. Often Don Antonio would visit them, bringing his small son. The two would listen wide-eyed, open-mouthed while Vaca related certain adventures in an effort to describe the many strange peoples and places they had visited. Hardest of all was trying to explain the different roles they had been forced to assume just to survive.

After such a visit from Mendoza, when they had been describing their years as slaves, Esteban asked the others if they thought the viceroy had understood the life they had endured. "Our talk only lasted about an hour," he commented, "how can our years be explained in so short a time?"

"It's like the dates on a gravestone—a lifetime," Castillo said. "Yet now I can look back and accept them as our reasonable term of apprenticeship. We did learn to be savages."

"You can't dismiss Esteban's question by talking about how *we* judge those years and that slavery," Vaca said. "How can Don Antonio understand? Often as I am talking, I wonder whether he understands what I am saying. Could any of us have understood if we had not experienced it? Just consider. Put yourself in Don Antonio's place. What could he know of poverty that would make it possible for him to picture that of the Arbadaos, for example?"

"If you put it that way, nothing. Hunger as well," Castillo added. "I'll wager the only hunger he has ever known is that of a fast day. And you want him to imagine hunger as the everyday condition of life? Impossible."

At a later visit Don Antonio listened with special attention when Vaca described the Indians they met just north of the region Guzmán had overrun. He had been unable to think of the simple hunting Indians as anything but animals; but he could picture the village-dwellers where a house was a house and not twigs woven together, and turtle-like, carried around from place to place. Vaca mentioned in happy remembrance the villages strung out along the length of an extensive, fertile valley; the gardens which yielded rich harvests of maize, squash, and beans; and the people decently clad in cotton blankets finer than those woven in New Spain.

The mention of the goods they obtained stirred the viceroy's interest. Gay parrot feathers had been traded for turquoises and emeralds with tribes to the north, tribes, Esteban had learned from questioning, whose towns were populous and filled with large, many-storied, stone houses. Between the village peoples and the turquoise nations was a barrier of harsh, barren mountains and a wide, arid, empty plain. But, Vaca assured the viceroy, they had been led over similar ranges where, as they walked, he had seen ample evidence of mineral wealth, of gold, iron, copper, and other metals.

"I am sure your eyes did not deceive you," the viceroy said, "since they are already mining gold and silver near Culiacán. It confirms the report Guzmán had from Indian traders that beyond the mountains are cities of great riches. True, he was unable, for all his efforts, to get through the mountains." Don Antonio paused a moment and then asked point-blank, "Does your information indicate whether the cities are *the* Seven Cities?"

"Your excellency," Vaca answered, choosing his words carefully, "we only *heard* about those cities. We never saw them. We got no idea of their number—only that they are many. However, neither the Indians' talk nor our not seeing them proves or disproves anything. For my part I am convinced that it is most likely that those are the Seven Cities. Anything is possible."

The viceroy was thoughtful. "Yes, in this New World anything is possible. While you were experiencing hardships, Cortés's cousin, Pizarro, following the stories of wealthy kingdoms, finally found Peru. It's a richer prize than his cousin's."

"If Pizarro's treasure was found far south of Mexico, it is logical that a still greater one lies north of Mexico," Vaca said with emphasis.

"Your excellency; Don Álvar," Castillo broke in, "if I may say a blunt word. Logic has nothing to do with geography or treasure. The ancients taught us that there is a vital connection between the planets and metals and that gold grows most plentifully where the sun is hottest —on either side of the equator. Both Mexico and Peru lie within the proper zone. The cities we heard about are out-side. I'll wager that they will be poor. I will add one word more: Don Antonio, the most promising region we saw would be most unpromising to your eyes."

"Unpromising? What do you mean?"

"I have been blunt; let me be precise, your excellency. Would it not be logical for Indians who have no per-manent houses to be awed by any building, to consider a well-built pigpen a palace? I remember how impressed I was at my first sight of permanent habitations. Yet the Cow People's entire settlement would fit in your excel-lency's courtyard. Forgive me, Don Antonio, if I cannot forget all we were told about the glorious kingdom of Apalache—and what did we find?"

"Are you saying that there are no more golden king-doms to be found?"

"No, Don Antonio. I am merely saying that I do not be-lieve in rumours. Or, it would be truer to say that I am through running after every rumour."

"I can understand your reluctance, Captain," the vice-roy said. "You have had much to discourage you." His voice was cold, as though he had crossed Castillo off some kind of list.

As soon as they were alone, Esteban asked, "What are the Seven Cities? The Indians never mentioned them."

"The Seven Cities have been spoken of for a long, long time," Vaca explained, hoping that his detailed an-swer would recall clues Esteban might have heard in his talks with the Indians. "When the Moors overran Spain, seven Portuguese bishops sought to save their people from the infidels. They put out to sea in boats and sailed west-

ward over the Ocean Sea. They found land far to the west
and established seven cities. We know that the fair, rich
cities they founded, prospered. The only thing we do not
know is where they are."

"Where. Exactly, Don Álvar, where. Forgive me if I
act the Devil's Advocate. In the university I saw maps
which placed the Seven Cities on islands—the Seven
Cities of Antilia. We now call those islands by other
names—Cuba, Santo Domingo, and so on. We found no
cities." Castillo's voice was excited. "I also remember that
the first Englishman to sight the New World claimed he
saw, actually saw, the Seven Cities. But he didn't bring
back its gold as Cortés did; he came home with a cargo of
fish."

"Alonso, I think I understand," Vaca said after a slight
pause. He was neither offended nor antagonized by the
younger man's outburst. "For you the quest is over; you
are through with the wilderness; you have come home to
stay. You think the Seven Cities are just another myth."

"As one of the Children of the Sun, I know a myth
when I see it. You are right, Don Álvar. I struggled to
come back. Now I am home." He was silent for a moment.
"Since this is a farewell, let me say that our wanderings
with their successful ending will remain memorable. I
am certain nothing I do will ever have the same high
quality. I will look back on it with wonder. I shall also
never again enjoy friendships as true and happy as I
had with you and Andrés and Esteban. Most men walk
through the worldly wilderness and become lost; we
walked through a real wilderness and there found what
it is to be human. This I shall cherish."

T HE SEVEN CITIES: the viceroy could think of nothing else. He had but to find them to win glorious renown by conquering new and rich empires for the king. Finding them was the problem. Castillo had announced he would not go seeking them. He still had Vaca and Dorantes to guide the way. They, too, had come from the north, conducted by Indians through mountains that had stopped Guzmán, whom nothing had ever stopped before. He would commission them to lead a small force there and establish contact with the Kingdom of the Seven Cities. He spoke to them separately.

Vaca had his own plans. Narváez's death had left him the legitimate successor to the governorship of La Florida. He was convinced that the Seven Cities lay within the grant of La Florida and he intended requesting that the King make his commission more than a piece of paper. Together, he told Dorantes, they could lead an expedition into the interior of La Florida where the kingdom lay. Castillo listened to their plan; repeatedly they asked him to join them, but he would not change his mind.

"It is ten years since I played my lute. I must learn how to make music again. I will be able to tell my lute about the wilderness." And then Castillo added seriously, "If the Seven Cities exist, you are the ones to find them."

"Don Álvar," Dorantes said, "it is ten years since Narváez perished. God rest his soul. Suppose you find that his commission has been given to another. I will never serve under another peacock."

"In that case, Andrés, we shall each do what we want to do. As of now I know that La Florida has not been granted to anyone else."

Soon after they had made this loose agreement, the viceroy approached Dorantes. As Vaca had before, so now Dorantes declined to lead an expedition for the viceroy. "I have decided," he told Don Antonio, "to return to Spain before taking on any new assignment. Let me be frank: Don Álvar Núñez and I have a project. But if it falls through—I think it most unlikely—I might be interested in your offer."

The viceroy saw his Seven Cities conquest recede into the unknown north: first Castillo, then Vaca, now Dorantes. Of the four only Esteban was left. Impulsively, for the dream of the Seven Cities overcame his natural caution, he said, "Captain, sell Esteban to me. I will pay a good price."

Stunned—how long was it since he had thought of Esteban as a slave, or Esteban thought of him as his master?—Dorantes managed to keep his manner correct. But his voice and words showed his bewilderment and indignation. "Your excellency has reminded me that Esteban is my property. I had quite forgotten that. He has been my friend for so long. Would I be here without him to give strength to my strength? Sell Esteban? The idea is unthinkable. I am no Judas; not for all the silver of the New World."

I must not take offence, Don Antonio thought, regretting his impulsiveness; the wilderness gives men strange ideas. Patience, patience and calm. As long as Vaca, Dorantes and, yes, Esteban are in New Spain, I may still secure one of them for my enterprise. Conquering the Kingdom of the Seven Cities will yet make me as great as

Cortés. So Mendoza's thoughts ran. The more he thought of Esteban, the more he seemed the best candidate. The black slave was intelligent and again and again Vaca had commented on Esteban's special gift in dealing with the Indians.

It was the fall of 1536. For two months they had been the guests of Mendoza; in that time the viceroy had failed to enlist the services of any of the four. Castillo remained behind when Vaca, Dorantes, and Esteban left Mexico City for Vera Cruz to get passage to Spain. The three spent that winter at the port city, their departure delayed by a series of deadly storms and many false starts on ships that proved rotten and leaky and returned to port. At last Vaca's ship sailed. But Dorantes and Esteban remained waiting for a ship. Increasingly they found themselves ill-at-ease at the way people stared at them and the silly questions they were asked. The wilderness had left them vulnerable to all the barbs and pitfalls of the fortune hunters.

A letter from Mendoza requesting them to return brought them back to Mexico City that spring. Again they were lodged in the palace; again the viceroy spoke guardedly of an exploring party. One thing had changed. Castillo, the first to repudiate the wilderness, had married. As was customary for a penniless conquistador, his wife possessed a modest fortune and an agreeable hacienda. Castillo's lute-playing made the couple welcome everywhere; establishing himself as a married man with property brought him back to normal, settled life.

Life in the palace made Dorantes more restless. He was

struggling to answer the questions each of the four had faced as soon as their quest was completed: What do I do now? Am I prepared to stay at home after many years as a savage? Castillo had given his answer and Vaca his. For the present Dorantes continued to dodge the issue. He waited—waited to hear from Vaca. And, if that arrangement should fall through, discreet reminders from Mendoza offered him the chance to return to the north. Undecided, unhappy, Dorantes sought to escape from the palace's pressures and formalities and, with Esteban, spent days roaming around the Aztec capital. Though battered and scarred, the city had enough of its former magnificence and might, its spacious plazas and thriving markets, to command their wonder and admiration. Neither Spain nor Morocco, they agreed, had a city to match the matchless Tenochtitlán, as the Mexicans called their lake-city.

They visited Castillo, newly established on his estate a little outside of the city. His lady was cordial, welcoming them as her husband's most special friends; she was hospitable and sympathetic, and her voice, though small, was true and sweet. Castillo played for them, and she would sing; happiness gave a joyous quality to their music. The four would sit and eat and talk and laugh; it was especially pleasant. The visits grew more frequent and lasted longer. Castillo's felicity and contentment were contagious.

And so the summer passed. Slowly, steadily, Dorantes thought less and less of returning to the Spartan life of the frontier and the hazards of exploring, and more of the

quieter, simpler triumphs of Castillo's stay-at-home adventure. This was his mood when he received the word from Vaca for which he had been waiting.

It was a brief note. In it Vaca related how he reached Spain a few weeks too late to succeed the long-dead Narváez—this post had just been given to one Hernando de Soto who, from a fortune amassed in Peru, could, like his predecessor, equip an imposing expedition for the discovery and colonization of La Florida. Vaca had declined de Soto's invitation to serve under him. Vaca was getting ready to sail to the provinces of the Rio de la Plata —the king had graciously named him governor. "I write all this to you, Andrés, so that you will understand that I am releasing you from our agreement. May *you* find the Seven Cities and become richer than Pizarro!"

"Where is the Rio de la Plata?" Esteban asked when he had finished reading the letter to him.

"In South America. Paraguay. Why do you ask?"

"Not even on the same continent as La Florida. Why do I ask? I could understand Vaca's wanting to explore La Florida. But this new place. Doesn't it tell you that Vaca will always head for the wilderness? For a nature such as his, the struggle itself is his kind of home."

"What has that to do with me?"

"Because you are at a crossroads—one path marked Castillo, the other, Vaca. When we finally arrived in the land of Christians and Spaniards, Castillo found what he had sought. Not Vaca—he continues to seek. I am sure that in Estremadura they have a saying about the difference between finders and seekers." And they both laughed; but they were sad, missing the homely wisdom Vaca had dosed them with.

"I envy Vaca's fire-and-steel nature," Dorantes said to Esteban. "I don't know if it's the fire or the steel I lack. I think I could live here happily, like Castillo."

"What will you tell his excellency?"

"It will be hard, but I never promised him anything. I'm grateful for that. These last months I've had the time and chance to learn something about myself."

"For example?" Esteban said encouragingly.

"For example, that there may be other things in life besides looking for the Seven Cities." There was no need for Dorantes to spell it out; they both knew to what he was alluding. He, like Castillo, had joined the Narváez expedition for adventure and for the fortune to be made in the New World. Of adventure, he was almost ready to admit, he had had enough to last him a lifetime; as for his fortune, he had found a surer, pleasanter way to achieve it. Doña Maria, a young widow whose husband had left her much wealth and rich lands, had confided to Castillo's wife that she favoured Dorantes above her other suitors.

"Andrés, what devil makes you hesitate? Why do you say *may be*? Was our quest nothing but a test of perseverance and endurance? Let Vaca seek glory. Let Mendoza crave glory. Glory, however, is like grace—God gives it; men can only recognize it. Marry. Marriage will bring you everything you wanted in the world you struggled to regain. At least let one of us be happy."

ONLY ESTEBAN WAS LEFT to lead Mendoza's party through the mountain barrier to the Seven Cities. Why he went and with whom, the manner of his going and what happened to him, are quickly told. What remains a matter to marvel at is how the separate dreams of a viceroy and a slave were joined in a bright adventure.

The viceroy's annoyance at Dorantes's marriage did not last long. Esteban remained with him in Mexico City and was still available to help Mendoza further his bid for fame and fortune. Before he could ask Esteban to find the path through the mountain barrier that blocked the way to the Kingdom of the Seven Cities, he had to deal with two men who were as formidable an obstacle. First there was Guzmán, governor of the northwestern frontier—but his day was over and soon he would be brought to account for his brutal misdeeds against Spaniards as well as Indians. Then there was the aging Cortés who, jealous of the only exploration rights left to him, would oppose any expedition sent toward the Seven Cities.

To circumvent them, the viceroy quietly, almost secretly, formed a plan and found the man to carry it out. Neither Guzmán nor Cortés would dare object to a religious mission. And as for the Indians, Mendoza thought, if they allowed the unarmed Children of the Sun to walk unharmed through the wilderness, why couldn't two or three friars advance as they preached? His plan was simple and foolproof; the more he considered it, the better it seemed. Instead of Vaca, I will send Fray Marcos. All I need is for Esteban to guide him. Delighted with his solution, Mendoza went ahead with his plans. Time was on his side. He did not rush into action but neither did he remain idle. He had found the Franciscan Fray Marcos through the bishop, who vouched for his being as learned in cosmography as in theology; and when he told the monk the plan, he was delighted that Marcos was eager to serve him. By the fall of 1538 all the parts were assembled and in readiness. It only remained for the viceroy to fit the keystone into his plan: Esteban.

Dorantes had been married almost a year when he was honoured by a visit from the viceroy. Behind him, his page carried a heavy, splendidly worked silver tray on which, in generous disorder, were five hundred silver coins.

"Don Andrés, I will come to the point," he said, after they had enjoyed a cup of foaming cocoa. "But first, may I ask that Esteban be sent for." When Esteban came into the room, Mendoza continued. "When I asked you to sell Esteban, I acted without understanding the special bond that unites you. Now I am talking to both of you. The tray and silver are for you both, as an earnest token of my penitence." The two men bowed in accepting it.

Mendoza continued. "I come to ask Esteban to guide the mission I am sending to the Kingdom of the Seven Cities. He will go, not as a slave, but as a companion to Fray Marcos, another friar, and some Christian Indians. There are to be no soldiers, only men dedicated to God and His Word. I want to show that the slave-catching raids of Guzmán are finished, and to send greetings and messages to the ruler of the Kingdom of the Seven Cities. His Catholic Majesty is deeply interested and approves of our efforts."

"Your excellency," Dorantes was speaking for both,

"we are greatly honoured. We must talk this over. We were not prepared for your offer; it is very sudden. You see, when I considered commanding your party, Esteban would have been with me. We have been together for more than ten years. We are like brothers. You will appreciate that his going alone is very different."

"I want you to talk it over." Mendoza was amiable. "Could I have your answer soon?"

"Don Antonio, you shall have it before the week ends."

"You will find Fray Marcos much to your liking. He too is a great walker—he walked here from Guatemala when the bishop summoned him. He is now his Grace's house guest."

Following the viceroy's hint, Dorantes invited Fray Marcos to visit him. He came at once. Mendoza had impressed on him the importance of securing Esteban.

When he was sitting with Dorantes and Esteban, he talked easily, the words pouring out, sometimes revealing, sometimes obscuring what he had to relate. "I lived for a time in Nice, that's why they call me Fray Marcos of Nice—we are so many Marcoses among the Franciscans," he explained lightly. "I have heard about you and your miraculous return; the matter of God's involvement in your cures is a most interesting theological problem. I hope you will tell me more when we return from our blessed mission." And he glanced significantly at Esteban.

"May I introduce myself? Let me tell you something about what I have done, where I have been. I'll start when I came to Santo Domingo as a missionary in thirty-one." And then he related the high points of his extraordinary travels and encounters. Talking rapidly, with wide gestures—once he picked up his skirts to show how he had scaled a steep cliff—he jumped from place to place, from event to event. Dorantes and Esteban listened spellbound, for Marcos seemed to have met the most important men and witnessed momentous doings.

In Guatemala—how did he get there? did he swim?—he met its conqueror, Alvarado, whose appetite for further conquests and greater loot was still unsatisfied, and with him went to Peru. Alvarado wanted to join the Pizarro venture, but the Pizarro brothers were not looking for partners. Somehow, it was not clear exactly how, Marcos left Alvarado and accompanied Francisco Pizarro on his overland march into Peru. He had been present on two noteworthy occasions: he had seen the callous execution of the Inca Atalhualpa. "When he had no more gold, Don Francisco said he was as useless as a sucked-out orange. I offered to save the Inca if he would be baptized, but he refused outright, saying he did not want to go to heaven, since it would be full of Christians." Remembering this, Fray Marcos shook his head sadly. Again and again he shuddered at other ungodly acts, such as the time he saw Alvarado sell his rights in the conquest of Ecuador to Almagro. Alvarado, he implied with a shrug of his shoulders and a roll of his eyes, had been paid in lead coin.

Was it the murder or the swindle that had soured Fray Marcos and decided him to leave Peru? When they talked over his visit, neither Dorantes or Esteban were quite sure.

"How much he was doing in the very years we were slaves," Dorantes said.

"Andrés, what do you think of him?"

"My head is still spinning with all the great names he mentioned. I would call him a braggart except that his bishop says he is reliable; he also vouches for his virtue and zeal." Dorantes paused, and then added, "Maybe it is his cleverness with words. You know I am not sure if he said what I think he did or if he led me to hear things he never put into words." And Dorantes shook his head, puzzled by Marcos's skill and deft way with words. "And you, Esteban?"

"I know what you mean. We are accustomed to the straightforwardness of Don Álvar's talk. But the trouble may be in the man, not his talk. Don Álvar was important in himself; Fray Marcos is self-important. A difference. Yes? In Azamor we would say of Marcos, 'We have ploughed the field.'"

Dorantes looked at Esteban, waiting for the explanation that would come.

"We have a bird that rides on top of oxen and catches the flies it attracts. And now that I am thinking of it, the bird's feathers are the same grey as Marcos's habit. Well, when an ox returns from the day's ploughing, the bird says proudly, 'We have ploughed the field.'"

"We have ploughed the field," Dorantes repeated, laughing. "Very appropriate. But what oxen! Our most successful conquistadors. I got the distinct impression that the good brother is more anxious to serve Mendoza than God."

"True, true. That is the reason he reminded me of Friar Juarez, God rest his soul. You remember Don Álvar's telling us how the friar, to please Narváez, silenced all criticisms made against the governor's plan?"

"Such obsequiousness in Mexico City is merely unpleasant," Dorantes said, "but in the wilderness it cost the lives of the expedition. I wonder if Mendoza chose the right person to carry God's word beyond the frontier."

"I do not question his religious zeal. But I do remember Lope who turned away from Don Álvar and went back into slavery. Marcos's walk into Peru with Pizarro is merely a test of his leg muscles; it is no test of his ability to go unarmed to the Seven Cities," Esteban said, and then, after a long pause, added quietly, "Andrés, we are in agreement about Marcos. But I shall go with him."

"What?" Dorantes's voice was as loud and sharp as a musket shot. "Are you crazy? Did I hear right? Why?" He floundered, trying to understand why Esteban, thinking as he did, should choose to go with Fray Marcos.

"Andrés, listen. Let me try to explain. What did I say when you had the same choice before? I said that you and Castillo had finished the quest; you were home. But that Vaca would go on seeking. Remember?"

"Yes," the word came slowly, reluctantly.

"We are like brothers—and yet we are not in the sense of having the same home. In the wilderness we could be slaves together, we could be Children of the Sun together —there was a quest to bring out our best qualities, there was a goal for which we could work together. That is over. What can I do now? I cannot return to Azamor—I am a Christian. I cannot return to Spain—I am not a Spaniard. Of course I can stay here with you—but this cannot be my home. Where, I ask you, is my home? This is what I am going to seek. In the heart of that great wilderness, I will find the home for men like me."

"Here is your home," Dorantes said, looking straight into Esteban's eyes.

"No Andrés, alas, no. I am not unhappy being with you, and Doña Maria is deeply understanding and accepts me as your family. But were you in my place, would you stay? Events have forced me to be a seeker, like Don Álvar. Like him, I shall go back to the wilderness. In all the years since I fled from Azamor, where else have I known the friendships and freedom I had there? Who knows what I shall find this time." He glanced at Dorantes, whose look of sad disbelief wiped all other expression from his face.

"I shall take the sacred rattle we used to announce the mission of the Children of the Sun. I shall faithfully observe all the ceremonies that were so fruitful, and the behaviour that made us respected by the Indians. Don't worry about Fray Marcos—he won't bother me. We are, the viceroy said, to be equals. I shall try to go on ahead, alone with the Indians, leading the procession that brings health and hope. I shall also prepare the groups we meet for the Fray's coming."

"To go as a Child of the Sun, naked, unarmed, is one thing; but to go guiding Mendoza's spy is quite another thing."

"That is a way of looking at it, Andrés. I consider the Kingdom of the Seven Cities as the talisman that unites Mendoza and Esteban in a common hope. It was the name my mother called me."

"Suppose the Kingdom of the Seven Cities has citizens utterly different from the groups we met. You might find death there, not home."

"I have thought of that, too. In that case I shall die as a Child of the Sun. Andrés," and his voice vibrated with his deep intensity, "don't try to keep me from going." After a moment he said in a lighter tone, "Accept my share of the silver tray and coins as a present to you and Doña Maria. For your home."

MARCH 1539: The birds were singing when the small party left Culiacán—Esteban, Fray Marcos, another Franciscan, Fray Onorato, and a dozen Indians set free by Mendoza. They carried the baggage of the two, religious gifts the viceroy was sending to the king of the Seven Cities as tokens of his friendship, and samples of pearls, precious stones, gold and silver that were to be shown to the Indians they met. Mendoza sought to insure that there would be no misunderstanding as to where these treasures abounded. Word of Esteban's coming went ahead, and Indians from the villages through which the four had passed came to meet He-Who-Speaks-for-the-Children of the Sun, who was returning to visit them.

They brought the wilderness back to him. Shedding his clothes, naked like the Indians, Esteban strode happily toward an uncluttered, unbroken land whose horizons beckoned him to freedom. And as Vaca had kept their path toward the setting sun, so now Esteban took his bearing from the polestar. In his hand he held the sacred rattle presented to the four far, far to the east, the rattle whose voice had spoken to all the tribes they had met, the rattle whose voice had always assured their welcome and their transit.

As though it had never stopped, the procession began again. Esteban explained its origin and importance to Marcos and Onorato who had been sceptical as to its purpose. Later, when he sounded the rattle, they feared it might be some form of idolatry. However, when they saw the Indians receive them with deference and treat them with reverence, they were reassured. The Indians sensed something special about the two men dressed in long grey habits, and knew instantly, without being told, that they were not Guzmán's raiders.

At first everything went well. The first misunderstanding arose on account of the many women in the escort. Marcos and Oronato looked at them severely; they fussed and worried at their presence and only reluctantly believed Esteban when he explained that they were the porters, leaving the men free to act as hunters and warriors.

"Alvarado and Pizarro also had women in their retinues," Fray Marcos said, his lips tight with disapproval. "They did not claim the women were porters; we had slaves who carried the equipment." He looked at Esteban reproachfully. "Fray Onorato and I cannot be expected to be party to debauchery. It would be a sin for us to travel with your harem."

Deeply offended, Esteban managed to control himself and answer with patience and dignity. "I am not one of your conquistadors. The Children of the Sun are different from them in every way. Because we knew God was with us, we were careful not to offend Him; because the Indians had faith in us, we were careful not to offend them. We were abstemious and continent. That was our custom and I continue it; to me it is more than a habit, it is a religious necessity. Do not imagine things, Fray Marcos, set your mind at rest."

Esteban thought, If I don't suspect him of tampering with women, why should he suspect me? He judges me from his previous experience with men like Alvarado and Pizarro. But I'll wager he never scolded them. Doesn't he know there are other ways of behaving? As Vaca said long ago, there are some things that you cannot be told or taught; they have to be learned by each man in his own way. The four of us learned from the wilderness. I'm afraid Mendoza did not choose his man well. Marcos's courage rests on his being allied with superior strength. Such a man walks delicately in the presence of the important and stamps on those he feels are inferior. I am sure Marcos will see what he is expected to see and will testify long and eloquently to please Mendoza.

On his side, Fray Marcos, who felt at ease with conquistadors, viceroys, and bishops, did not feel comfortable with a black man who, despite everything Mendoza had said, was a slave. What made it strangely threatening was that this man was as fine-grained as any of the Spaniards. He accepted the respect the Indians showed him and gave it back to them enhanced by his manner. As long as Marcos had the companionship of Onorato, his essential weakness did not show itself. But within the first fortnight Onorato sickened, and as his illness in-

creased daily, it was decided to send him back to Culiacán.
Sorrowfully Marcos watched the Indians make a litter to
carry him back along the trail they had just come. When
he saw it disappear from sight, he turned to Esteban.

"He is very ill, very weak. I tremble for his life. Will
he be safe all alone with the Indians?"

"Console yourself, Fray Marcos. You need have no
worries for his safety. He is a holy man; they will tend
and care for him. If God spares him, he will reach Culiacán." Even as Marcos was expressing fears for Onorato,
Esteban knew that it was Marcos himself who was in
need of reassurance. From now on, each forward step
would take him farther and farther from their base at
Culiacán. From now on he was alone with Esteban and
the Indians.

One night, soon after, when they sat by the fire talking
after their one daily meal, Esteban sensed Marcos's mounting apprehensions. As if to calm his own fears, Marcos
related his brave, solo walk from Guatemala to Mexico:
He walked through country newly pacified. He kept repeating how different that march was from this. These
Indians, who seemed so obedient and gentle, had not yet
submitted to Spanish rule; and what would the Indians
be like when they left these settled villages and moved
among hunting groups? His fears grew with each mile
they put between them and Culiacán. His eyes, Esteban
thought, are getting the look of a trapped animal.

Fray Marcos was in the grip of two powerful emotions:
fear and ambition. As each step carried him farther and
farther into the unknown, he knew how sailors must have
felt when, thinking the world was flat, they never knew

when the ship would fall over the edge of the earth. But he also burned with the gambler's passion, the driving force to find mighty stores of gold, the same lust that had driven Pizarro and Alvarado and all the lesser fortune hunters. The thrill of high stakes pushed him forward toward the Seven Cities.

The procession moved slowly because at each village Marcos stopped to show the Indians he met the samples he had with him. The first day he showed them a cross, a wooden crucifix tipped with silver. And when the Indians responded, nodding their heads and pointing to the west, he was certain that he had only to go in that direction to stumble on a silver mine. He found himself disliking Esteban when the black man spoiled his dream, telling him that it was the cross the Indians recognized and not the silver, and that their pointing to the west referred to the direction taken by the Children of the Sun.

"Fray Marcos," Esteban said one night, coming straight to the matter, "would it please you more if I went ahead to scout the way while you took all the time you want to check thoroughly on possible treasure to be found? I will provide a buhío for your comfort at the end of each day's march; your coming will be awaited and food will be on hand for you. When I have sighted the, kingdom, I will return as soon as I have prepared them for your arrival." Clearly, they had not been happy together. Esteban knew that since the wilderness had not brought them close in friendship, it would be easier for each if they separated and each advanced when and as he wanted to.

Two days before Passion Sunday, they came to a large village whose inhabitants went regularly to the not-too-distant Pacific coast. When Fray Marcos showed them pearls, they said such things were easily and plentifully found on an island near the coast. Marcos decided to wait there while they brought some of the island Indians for him to question. Also, he told Esteban, he felt safe in the village; the inhabitants addressed him as *Sayota*, Man from Heaven.

They parted the Sunday before Easter. Esteban, carrying his sacred gourd, led the procession out of the village. Before him lay the wide desert, and somewhere beyond that, Cíbola. Cíbola was the Indian name for the Kingdom of the Seven Cities. At last the goal had a name, it existed; it was not merely a legend of nomadic Indians.

They would never see each other again.

SOMEWHERE ESTEBAN and his escort crossed a boundary; he never knew exactly where. Was it somewhere along the vast plain, gashed with dry arroyos, which they had crossed in ten forced marches? For ten days they had walked through a monotonous landscape of sage and yucca, cacti and stunted, thorny mesquite; for ten days they had walked under a blazing June sun and at night had huddled close to fires to keep away the cold that gripped that open, high plateau. A wind sweeping the dry earth had filled their mouths and clogged their nostrils with grit. Then, suddenly, their march was finished; the wind died down, far to the east they saw pine-covered mountains; and before them a lake. It was like a benediction. Spring-fed, its water was deliciously fresh and cold and sweet.

It was no ordinary lake. Along its edge feathered sticks, blue and yellow, stood side by side, while here, there, and everywhere were black ones. Small, straight, carefully smoothed and painted, each stick was adorned with feathers attached by a cotton cord. Esteban noticed that each stick had been carefully sprinkled with meal. Looking at it, he knew that it could only be food for the gods, made of a mixture of maize, white shells, and turquoises coarsely ground. The trail they had followed had brought them to Whispering Spring, the pond sacred to the Zuni Indians. Not far off was one of the settlements the outsiders had called Cíbola; the Zuni themselves called it Háwikuh.

Esteban looked long and carefully at the lake, the feathered sticks, the sprinkled meal. All these things were utterly new and different; all announced that he had crossed a boundary. With that thought came another: Will death mark its crossing?

He could not retreat. He knew that even if he could have turned back, he would not. He could not halt the procession's forward movement, for the myth decreed that life itself was guaranteed to all who walked in the company of He-Who-Speaks-for-the-Children of the Sun. Suddenly his thoughts were stopped by the feeling of apprehension that seized the Indians at the sight of alien customs; the very sound of Cíbola had a threatening quality. Their fears opened a dark door. Esteban remembered the temples he and Andrés had visited in their

walks around the Aztec capital. The steep steps leading
to the altars were brown and stinking from dried blood
of hundreds of human hearts snatched red and warm and
still beating from captives. Food for the gods; food to
feed the sun, they had been told. Did the gods of Cíbola
also need human blood to live?

Soon enough, he thought, I will know whether I have
come this long way, all the way from Azamor, to die here
at Cíbola. Each of us goes as far as he can. Until I have a
successor, I shall have seen what no other man from the
Old World has yet seen. It is a very small achievement,
but still an achievement. He smiled and his smile reassured
the Indians with him.

He spoke to those near him. "Wait here. I will go with
my sacred rattle and speak with the men of Cíbola."

With only an Indian on either side, Esteban walked the
few miles to the settlement. The afternoon was old when
they reached it—not the city he had dreamed of, but what
looked in the slanting sun's rays like a few houses
cramped together. In front of a house that stood apart,
outside the village, six men awaited him. Impressive in
dress and bearing, masters of a quiet authority, they were
the council of priests who regulated the life of their
people.

The council was expecting him. Long before the procession had reached the sacred pool, Zuni scouts had kept it
under surveillance. For an incredible moment they looked
at one another—these dwellers of an unknown outpost
of the ancient pueblo way of life with its known gods and
calendar, its priests and rituals, and the intruder, this
unlikely representative of the Old World. Then, before

speaking any words, Esteban sounded his rattle to announce that his was a mission of peace and of supernatural power.

Almost instantly, one of the priests stepped forward, seized the rattle and threw it violently to the ground as though it were an enemy, repeating over and over again, "Piro, Piro." A moment later the other priests beckoned Esteban to come toward them. Leaving his companions, he stepped forward, alone. Flanked by the priests he faced the house just outside the pueblo. Before entering it through the hatchway in the roof, he turned and motioned to the two Indians who had accompanied him to return to the lake. He remembered how the procession would not leave the Children of the Sun when they had met the Spaniards. He prayed that they would return to Fray Marcos. What ever happens to me will happen, he thought, but no harm must come to the Indians who trusted me.

Esteban was in a kiva. Feathered prayer sticks and sprinkled sacred meal told him that it was a kind of temple, a place for holy ceremonies. It was the very first temple he had seen in all his wanderings through the wilderness. Unlike those of Mexico, it was not set atop a lofty pyramid—a reassuring fact. Though the kiva was almost on ground level, its overhead entrance made it seem like a cave opening into the darkness and silence of the earth. Gradually his eyes grew accustomed to the twilight gloom; the intense quiet of the kiva flowed over him. How peaceful it is, he thought, and was suddenly reminded of the dark, enclosing security he had known as a child when his mother held him close. Can it be that so far from Azamor I have come home?

Uppermost in his mind was the need to get back to tell Andrés what Cíbola was. Fray Marcos will never see Cíbola to know the truth. He will never tell the truth—he hasn't it in him.

The stillness and inaction after his driving spurt northward, his reaching Cíbola, and his overwhelming disappointment at its smallness and meanness, suddenly left him utterly spent and tired. "I have gone far enough," his body told him.

He slept, each move, each sound, watched over by vigilant eyes.

For four days and four nights the council of priests searched their assembly of supernaturals and found no way to reconcile him with any of these; nor could they place him in the calendar which governed their year. They fed him as they would a god, sprinkling the holy meal of maize, shell, and turquoise down the opening of the temple. Always, the Bow Priests reported, he sat in the kiva where the passage of night and day was a change from brilliant starlit darkness to a sunless dusk, and neither sang nor danced.

Out of their thoughts and wisdom came their decision: He was Dark Star Man, one of the Great Ones, a messenger from the ancients in the underworld. Before he could entice any of the living to follow him to the village under the lake called Whispering Spring, he must be sent back to the Koko village. Had he come when the rainmakers were expected, they would have honoured him with singing and dancing. Alas.

On the fourth day, while he slept, they stabbed him with a sharp stone knife. And because his body was sacred, it had to be totally destroyed so that it could not return to life and, as an evil spirit, follow them into their homes. As the wisdom of the ancients decreed, Esteban's body was cut into many small pieces which were taken to the four directions so that they would never come together. When it was done, the Bow Priests went through the necessary purification ceremony.

It is all finished.

Just as breakfast cereals list what they contain, so, I think, should a book presented as "historical fiction"—as is *The Gentle Conquistadors*. The reader has a right to know which parts are historical and can be verified, and which are out of the author's imagination. Let us begin with the historical ingredients.

We know about the Narváez expedition and the transcontinental walk of the four from the survivors themselves. So, there are primary sources. First, the *Joint Report*, which was written by the four for the viceroy, Don Antonio. Though the original is missing, a summary of it was included in Oviedo y Valdes' *La Historia general de las Indias* published in 1535. Second in point of time but first for its prime importance is Vaca's *Relacíon*, the account he wrote himself for His Sacred Caesarian Catholic Majesty, Charles V. It was first published in Zamora in 1542. This, as well as the accounts written by Fray Marcos and by Pedro de Casteñada, who took part in a later expedition, can be read in *Spanish Explorers in the Southern United States, 1528–1543, Original Narratives of Early*

American History, edited by Frederick W. Hodge and Theodore H. Lewis, published in 1907.

Of the vast number of secondary sources, I will only mention two: A. S. Aiton's biography of the viceroy, *Antonio de Mendoza, conde de Tendilla, 1491–1552* and *Álvar Núñez Cabeza de Vaca: The Journey and Route of the First European to Cross the Continent of North America*, in which Professor Cleve Hallenbeck describes how, using Vaca's *Relación,* he identified and followed the still-traceable Indian trails taken by the four.

The Narváez expedition and its heroic sequel—an important step in the exploration of the southern United States by Spaniards—occurred after Cortes's conquest of Mexico, and before the famous expeditions of Coronado and de Soto probed deep into the lower third of the United States. It is impossible to consider Coronado's venture without recognizing the accomplishment of his precursors. Because Castillo and Dorantes sank into a happy oblivion and Vaca's subsequent efforts were in South America, it is Esteban—who journeyed from Mexico City to the New Mexico-Arizona line where the Zuni pueblo of Háwikuh was located—who truly pioneered the Spanish advance into the United States.

Who was Esteban? Though his was a critical role, the facts about him are few and stark. We know only his Christian name, his birthplace, and that he was the slave of Dorantes. No more. We do not know if he was an Arab or Negro or, as Winship (*The Coronado Expedition, 1540–1542*) calls him, the "Arab negro from Azamor."

Such empty spaces invite the imagination. Here, then,

is the fiction ingredient. I gave Esteban a family and a childhood. For the fate of Azamor which started his travels, I have relied on a contemporary account of that part of Africa, *The history and description of Africa, and of the notable things therein contained, written by al-Hassan ibn-Mohammed al-Wezaz al-Fasi, a Moor baptised as Giovanni Leone, but better known as Leo Africanus* (translated into English in 1600 by John Pory). Leo Africanus wandered about Morocco during the very years of Esteban's life in Azamor and his book provided the material for my fiction.

However, for Esteban's character and talents we have Vaca's references to the years they lived together in the wilderness. I have merely made explicit what was implicit in the *Relacíon*.

For Esteban's journey northward from Mexico City, *we have only Fray Marcos's words.* Let me summarize his report after the ill Fray Onorato had been sent back. On March 21, two days before Passion Sunday, Marcos and Esteban reached a large village. Rumours of pearls found on an island in what is now the Gulf of California demanded verification. Marcos decided to remain there to question Indians summoned from the coast. On Passion Sunday, Esteban went ahead "to see if it was possible to learn of something grand." He was, Marcos wrote, to probe some one hundred fifty miles and send back reports. If he learned of a noble kingdom he was either to return or send back a messenger and await Marcos's arrival. Since Esteban could not write, they agreed on a code: for a moderately important country, the messenger would bring a white cross, a palm in length; for a country of great importance, a cross two palms long; and for "something greater and better than New Spain, he should send a large cross." After Passion Sunday each man was on his own. *Only Marcos returned to tell what happened.*

Four days later, Esteban's messengers staggered back carrying a man-high cross. They begged Marcos to hurry forward. "The greatest country in the world" lay—so an Indian who went there to trade had told Esteban—"thirty days' travel from the place where Esteban then was to the first city of the country, which is called Cíbola." Seven cities in the land of Cíbola—and the trader had described houses of stone and mortar. "On the doors of their principal houses," he further related, "there were many decorations composed of turquoise stones, of which there is great abundance in the land." Marcos did not rush forward. He waited until April 8 for the Indians from the Pearl Island. He sent word for Esteban to stay where he was until he, Marcos, joined him.

When at last he took the trail to catch up to Esteban, he was still in no hurry. First he verified an Indian report that the western coast suddenly turned sharply to the west. Did he actually make a side trip of about four hundred miles, or did he again send Indians to see for him? His account is fuzzy and vague. Before him was the Despoblado, the name given to the vast uninhabited region whose crossing required fifteen days. Though Esteban continued to push on, and though, as Marcos wrote, "each day seemed to me a year, on account of my desire to see Cíbola," Marcos did not begin the crossing until May 9.

Twelve of the fifteen days had passed when an Indian "all bloody and with many wounds" brought the dreadful news of Esteban's death and the massacring of his party. Only three out of more than three hundred had escaped alive! Everyone including Fray Marcos wept "from pity and fear." In spite of this disaster, Marcos was determined to see Cíbola for himself. Overcoming his fear—not for his life, he explained, but lest his glorious news perish with him—he advanced to a hill whence he saw the city. The land was "the largest and best of all those discovered." He stayed long enough to take formal possession for the viceroy and Spain, erecting two crosses, and then turned and hurried back "with much more fear than food." It was this news of another Mexico, another Peru, that sent Coronado out to conquer Cíbola.

Coronado was the first to call Marcos a liar. In the brief, bitter dispatch written to the viceroy immediately after his men had forced their way into a small, mean pueblo—the mighty and wealthy city which Marcos had described so minutely and eloquently—he said, Marcos "has not told the truth in a single thing." Casteñado, who was also there, remembered that the Spaniards cursed the Fray for his falsehoods. Later historians who question Marcos's report of his journey excuse his inflated picture of Cíbola by saying that his eagerness made him see what he wanted to see. (Just as his ears heard Cíbola when the Indians talked of Shíwona, the Zuni name for their land.) Nevertheless, when Marcos talks about Esteban many believe him and accept Marcos's statement that Esteban's greed to possess turquoises and women prompted

the Indians to kill him. The historians did not pay suffi-
cient attention to the schooling in Indian life and ways as
related by Vaca. The large number of women who were
among the hundreds of Indians in Esteban's party were
not Esteban's harem—they were the carriers, while the
men were hunters. They were, alas, more like the thousand horses and mules which Mendoza supplied to the
336 men in the Coronado expedition to transport their
baggage and equipment.

A belief in Esteban's "harem" had its origin not in any
verifiable fact but rather in attitudes which cannot grant
heroic qualities to a black man and slave. Bluntly, I prefer
my imagination, formed by anthropological material, to
Fray Marcos's suspicions.

Historians' prejudices can be seen in another instance,
an important though small instance. In giving the proper
setting for the Coronado expedition, they say that the
viceroy *bought* Esteban from Dorantes and that it was
in the service of this new master that Esteban went with
Fray Marcos. Yet the viceroy's biographer (Aiton: p. 119)
wrote that Esteban was "not sold as is usually stated in
the histories which treat of this period," and quotes a
sixteenth-century chronicler (Baltazar de Obregon, *Cro-
nica, April 16 and 18*; published in 1584). Dorantes, the
latter wrote, "experienced deep grief on being asked that
Estebanico serve the viceroy, Don Antonio, and would
not give him up for 500 pesos on a plate of silver which
the viceroy sent as payment by a third person, but was
willing that Esteban serve the viceroy in the name of His
Majesty without payment because of the good which

might accrue to the souls of the Natives of those provinces and to the interests of the *real hacienda* [royal colony]." In *The Gentle Conquistadors* I omitted the "third person" and let the viceroy deal directly with Dorantes—I kept the meaning intact. This is how I believe "historical fiction" works.

Supported in my belief that Esteban went northward of his own free will because he found being a black man and a slave—even with the best of masters—unendurable in Mexico, and knowing that Marcos lied about Cíbola, I have not used what Marcos wrote about Esteban after they parted. For me, anthropological insights have a greater truth than the story Marcos used to explain Esteban's death to himself as well as to his Spanish contemporaries.

And so, dear readers (as they used to say in the old-fashioned novels), I hope I have explained what I mean by "historical fiction" and why my version of Esteban's death is in keeping with his courage and dignity as glimpsed in Vaca's *Relacíon*.

My friends have been most generous in their help and most encouraging in their interest. I would like to express warm thanks to Alfred L. Bush, Curator of the Princeton Collection of Western Americana, for his devotion to Esteban and his bibliographical suggestions; to Professors David Crabb and Alfonso Ortiz, of the Program in Anthropology at Princeton University, the former for his knowledge of Negro Africa, the latter for his rich insights into Pueblo ethnology and his advice on the Zuni reaction to Esteban's arrival at Háwikuh; to Gillett G. Griffin, Curator of Pre-Columbian Art, Princeton University Museum, and through his superb collection of children's books, a guide into that special world of story-telling; and to Catherine H. Sweeney, whose interest and high competence in botany served me in several critical places. I am especially grateful to my good friend Morris Philipson, Director of the University of Chicago Press, who gave me the chance to formulate my ideas about Esteban in an article, "Zeroing in on a Fugitive Figure: The First Negro in America," that appeared in *Midway*, June 1967.

Jeannette Mirsky

Princeton, New Jersey